C000140470

Copyright © May 2021 by Brenda Trim
Editor: Chris Cain
Cover Art by Fiona Jayde

* * *

If you put your mind to anything that you dream, you can achieve it!

CHAPTER 1

"*T*his isn't working. I'm still like that kid in Harry Potter that keeps blowing everything up." I sound like a whiny teenager, too, rather than a forty-five-year-old hybrid witch.

I couldn't help it. I was failing at everything. I was anxious and on edge while we waited for the other shoe to drop. A few months ago, I faced the powerful Fae Queen and managed to injure her and send her fleeing when she tried to kill me. No one knows how I pulled that off, but we all agreed she would be back seeking revenge for what I did to her.

"You will get the hang of it," Camille reassured me.

My witch mentor had suggested that I try my hand at potions so I could open a booth at S&S, the magical flea market our town held in the park in the town square. I didn't need the money, thanks to my Grams, but I needed the distraction, and all of my friends agreed it was the best way for me to get to know the supes in town.

For me, it was a toss-up between developing relationships

with others like me and finding a way to settle my nerves. Always being on edge was making me jumpy and my magic even more unreliable than usual. I survived on coffee, which might be partly responsible for my jitters, but caffeine overload could only explain so much.

Being addicted to the elixir of the Gods for three decades or so meant my body was immune to a large degree.

"I'm not so sure about that. I spent a life as a norm without an ounce of magic. Maybe I lost my connection to my power." I had no idea how any of this worked. I was learning, but my knowledge was that of a five-year-old when it came to anything supernatural.

Camille shook her hand and dumped the sludge out of my cauldron into the trashcan she'd poured salt into before we began. The substance would neutralize any lingering power. It would also keep me safe when I cast my circle of power. Who knew it was so utilitarian?

Camille gestured to the hefty tome sitting open on the long wooden worktable. "That's not possible. I sense something else is at work here; I just can't put my finger on it. Grab your family, grimoire."

That perked my ears. This was the first time Camille mentioned anything of the sort. I wondered what I was missing. Likely a whole lot, given that I had no idea what normal was. "What do you mean? Why haven't you said something before?"

"I wasn't sure until we got into more detailed work like this. I haven't come across anyone quite like you, so I dismissed my concerns at first. Let's see if there's anything to it."

I set the book in front of us and flipped it open. "I've only looked through this thing a couple of times. What am I searching for?"

"Anything Isidora would have written about you or your birth."

"I've never come across anything about me personally. I've only seen spells and potions. I wish the book would just show me what I'm looking for." My fingers tingled and the wind whipped through the room, blowing my hair around my face. The pages fluttered in the book then stopped about three-quarters through.

Eyes wide, I gaped at the grimoire then at Camille. "What's this?" Camille picked up an envelope and held it between her thumb and forefinger.

"I've never seen it before." I took it from her and noticed the way my hand was shaking. Taking a deep breath, I opened the flap and took out a handwritten letter.

"It's addressed to me." I checked the envelop and realized I'd missed my name on the outside.

"I bet it's from Isidora. What does it say?" Camille was right. The signature at the bottom was from my Grams. My eyes returned to the top of the page, and I hesitated in reading it. I suddenly wished Sebastian was there with me. This was one of those moments I knew would change my life —kind of like when I boarded the plane to England to attend my Gram's funeral.

Bas, my sort-of boyfriend, barely left my side for weeks. He'd refused to share my bed with me and had taken up residence on my sofa. He left when Camille told him we would be making potions. I assumed that he returned to his home in the nearby woods, but I had no idea. I could call him but decided against it.

Instead, I typed in a message to Violet and Aislinn, my two best friends. My girls should be here with me. "Violet and Aislinn will be here soon. Let's see what Grams had to say."

Camille nodded her head but said nothing. "My dearest,

Fiona. If you're reading this, that means I have passed on from this life." I read aloud, but my voice drifted off as I continued in silence. My heart raced when I read her apology for keeping my heritage from me for so long.

"What's a *nicotisa?*"

Camille's composure slipped, and her jaw dropped open. "Why are you asking? What does it say?"

"It says she and my mother bound my power shortly after I was born because they realized I was a *nicotisa*. That's why my mom moved away from the area, so it would be easier to hide me."

"That explains why she and your father left so abruptly. I never understood why they moved halfway across the world. Your father's career never meant that much to him before." Camille was tapping the table with a finger while she talked. I placed my hand over hers.

"Hellooo," Aislinn called out from downstairs in a singsong.

"We're up here," I called out.

"Okay, so what was so important you had me close the shop early for lunch?" Violet's voice echoed up the stairs before they entered the room.

I quickly explained what they'd missed then continued reading. "It's important that you call upon my spirit so I can assist you in understanding your transition." A little late for that, Grams.

"How does she propose you do that?" Camille leaned over and scanned the page and seemed to answer her question as she nodded. "She's brilliant. Even dead, she's breaking the rules and pushing limits."

I turned my head to glance at my mentor. "What do you mean?"

"Isidora had a knack for doing the impossible, even if it went against traditional convention," Camille explained.

Aislinn crossed the room and read from the other side of me. "And, she didn't know what the word impossible meant. She believed there was always a way. You just needed to consider a problem or spell from all angles."

Violet held up one finger. "Don't forget the most important part...you have to think outside the box."

Camille turned and started grabbing jars from one of the bookshelves. "I have no idea how she accomplished this, but she details here how we need to brew a potion of eyebright, cinnamon, mugwort, African violet, and Arabic gum, among other ingredients."

Most of the items on the list were familiar, but I never in a million years would have considered putting them together like this. "Witches use eye of newt and the spleen of eels? What happens with the potion? Because this combination sounds awful."

Violet laughed. "I wouldn't want to be you, that's for sure."

"Wait. What do you mean? Why wouldn't you want to be me?" My words came out so fast that I wasn't sure anyone could understand me.

Aislinn clapped my shoulder. "Because you get to drink this once you finish."

My head was shaking side to side before I replied. "Nope. I'll pass."

Camille pegged me with a stern look. "I have no idea what Isidora had to do to tether her soul to this plane, but I can tell you it required a sacrifice to keep from crossing the veil to the other side. I won't let that be for nothing."

I swallowed the lump in my throat. "No. You're right. Let's get to cooking."

"This is all you," Violet exclaimed as she helped grab ingredients and placed them on the table.

"I can't. I'll blow it up. It's what I've been doing for hours today." I looked at Camille, who had the gall to chuckle.

"You have to do this on your own," Camille told me. "Remember, patience and careful measurements. Establishing the right balance is the most important aspect when brewing."

Aislinn read off the ingredients, and Camille or Violet handed the correct jar to me, and I poured or scooped the requisite amount and dumped it into the cauldron. Next, I added the fire necessary to heat the elements and blend them while stirring counterclockwise.

The liquid bubbled and boiled. I barely held the bile back as I glanced into the pot and saw a dark green formula with chunks floating along the surface. My hand moved the wooden spoon while I tried not to breathe through my nose. It smelled worse than it looked.

I had no idea how I was going to get this crap down. I remember not wanting to eat Brussel sprouts when I was a kid. Now I liked them. Somehow, I didn't think this was going to be one of those acquired tastes.

"How will I know when it's ready?"

Camille looked over the potion my Grams had left me. "When it turns pink."

"I must have done something wrong. I doubt this murky mixture is changing…" my words trailed away when the chunky pieces melted into the liquid, and it started changing with every swirl of my spoon.

"Damn, I love magic," I exclaimed and scooped a spoonful of what looked closer to a strawberry margarita than anything magical if you ignored the sparks shooting off the top.

"It comes in handy," Violet agreed.

I brought the spoon to my lips and had to breathe through my mouth when the putrid odor hit me. It might look tasty now, but it smelled like crap. Before my mind could psych me out, I poured a large serving down my throat.

My throat instantly closed off, and I couldn't get any oxygen into my lungs. Next, it flooded my esophagus and gushed into my gut like a torrent. Fire exploded and encompassed me from head to toe. At the same time, I noticed the stuff tasted like an earthworm on the side of the road, rotting in the sun.

After several agonizing minutes, I shook my head and saw Violet and Aislinn hovering close to me. "I'm okay." It came out as more of a croak than anything else. I reached for a glass of water, but Camille snatched it away from me with a shake of her head.

"You can't drink anything. You never know how other substances will interfere with a potion."

I grimaced. "Why can't this taste better?"

"All magic requires a price. Potions hurt and make you sick." I blinked and looked at Camille. Couldn't she have mentioned that sooner? How the hell did she expect me to sell shit to people without knowing this? I'd have customers constantly complaining and wanting their money back.

"It's time to recite the spell." Aislinn's voice brought me out of my ruminations.

"Right." I focused on the letter and my grandmother's words when I noticed that I was glowing blue. At least you know you did the potion right.

"Let my voice be heard on the other side,

And reach the one tethered to my side.

Ignore the bounds of physics and give form to the formless

By the laws of our ancient craft, so mote it be."

The wind kicked up and blew out the candles. Outside, thunder cracked, and the clouds opened up. Rain pelted the window as streams of blue energy left my fingers to form a cyclone on the other side of the attic.

I shielded my eyes from the worst of the maelstrom and watched through the cover created by my arms. The light coalesced into the form of a person. When the wind died down, I lowered my hands and saw a figure I never thought I'd see again.

"Grams!" I rushed to her side and threw my arms around her. They traveled right through her body, leaving me trembling from the cold.

"It's about time you called to me, child. What took you so long?"

I thrust my hands on my hips and narrowed my eyes. "Sorry, but I was blindsided by the whole witch-Fae hybrid thing. Then I was attacked and almost killed by the Fae Queen. And before that, I had to find the portal then learn how to keep Fae from crossing to earth. A little heads up would have been nice!"

I was beyond glad to have her back and hadn't realized until that moment how angry I was for being kept in the dark. That took precedence.

Aislinn cleared her throat. "Don't forget that you had to get your grimoire back from Filaron before any of that."

"That little weasel stole my grimoire?" Grams turned red around the edges. She'd been glowing light blue and transparent, but when she growled in anger, she changed. Her form was solidified somewhat and had a red tinge around the edges.

"I wouldn't call him little, but he is a weasel." I lifted one shoulder. Filarion was a low-life thief. A good-looking one, but still an opportunist at heart.

"All that matters now is you managed the spell, and I'm here with you. Camille, good to see you. I need you and

Aislinn and Violet to help cast a spell to dissipate Fiona's energy signature."

Camille leveled a look at Grams that said she was upset. I wondered if it was because it pissed her off that Grams hadn't told her who or what I was. Or if it was something else. "I've told you before, Isidora. I'm not an idiot, regardless of what you might think. I was planning on tackling the topic after I taught your granddaughter to make potions. I'd bet that's why the Fae Queen targeted her. She'd like to steal her power along with the portal. But I want to know how you managed to come back without crossing over."

"Yeah, she's all about being the most powerful being alive. Imagine how your fight would have gone and what she would be like if she had an energizer battery inside," Aislinn pointed out.

"I have no idea what you just said. Please explain this to me. And how I can keep my friends safe. Attacks have happened ever since you guys started hanging out with me and the Fae came to live at Pymm's Pondside with me. I don't want to be the reason anyone is hurt." I had enough guilt riding me at the moment.

"That's nonsense. You're not responsible for that foul being's power-hungry ways. What is important to understand is that right now, you are like a nuclear reactor. You give off a signal that is impossible for supernaturals to miss or resist." My grams floated around the room as she spoke. That was going to take some getting used to, but I had her back!

"This is because I'm a *nicotisa*, right? What exactly does that mean?"

"And, how did you find out? She moved away when she was five years old? And, don't think I forgot about wanting to know how you are here with us now." There was a biting edge to Camille's tone of voice. It was clear she didn't get along all that well with my grandmother. There was a story there. I didn't have the mental faculties to get into it at the moment.

Grams glared at Camille then turned a smile on me. "We knew you were different the second you were born. It started when you were born with an energy that helped soothe your mother. And, I knew for certain when you summoned your bottle one day when I was watching you while your mother operated her booth at S&S. And, to answer your question. I wasn't certain I would make this work, but I bound my spirit to Fiona. I wasn't sure it would work. I couldn't find anything about casting a spell while astral projecting. I had to cast a spell on my soul, not my body."

The thought of having my grandmother's body tied to me turned my stomach, but that registered behind the rest of what she said.

"Okay." I wish I could summon things now.

I was in desperate need of a cup of high-octane bean juice if I was going to get through this conversation. Or maybe a shot or ten of tequila. My head was already starting to pound, warning me I needed caffeine. My ability to focus and engage in conversation went downhill fast if I ignored it.

Violet smacked my arm. "You don't understand. This is huge. We don't come into our powers until our twenties. Otherwise, it would be impossible to hide our existence. Can you imagine your kids calling ice cream or toys to them as you walked through stores?"

Grams bobbed her head up and down. "That wasn't due to your *nicotisa* distinction, though. That gives you the ability to cast magic on your own without needing to call on the elements, and your Fae side amplified that. When you were three, I cast a spell on you that diluted your power. Your parents felt you got too much attention from the Fae and decided to move away shortly before your sixth birthday."

That sounded ominous. And fit with what had been happening since I returned to Pymm's Pondside a few months ago. Honestly, my head was swimming, and I had a hard time comprehending everything. The last few months had prepared me for the insane. The mythical was real, and I was part of that world. Otherwise, I'd have checked myself into the loony bin.

"Let's dissipate her signature," Camille interjected as if she read my mind. Violet, Aislinn, and Camille gathered around me. Camille cast a circle of salt, enclosing all of us, then they muttered, "*Sors.*"

Share? I was learning Latin thanks to my new witchy side, but their choice of spell made no sense. "Why not *dissipo* or *dispergo?*"

"Because we are sharing your signature." I gaped at Aislinn's announcement.

Grams sighed and floated in front of me. "That's only the first step. I can see you've already cast protection spells over you and Pymm's Pondside. Those wards will now be far more effective."

"Didn't you hear me? I don't want to put them in any more danger!" I didn't mean to snap at Grams, but I refused.

Grams put her hands on her hips in that way she always did and pinned me with a glare. It was a look that took me back decades and reminded me of what it felt like to be punished by her.

I wanted to squirm under my grandmother's attention. "You aren't placing them in any more danger. I just hope we aren't shutting the barn door after the horse got out. The Queen already has you in her targets, but this will stop anyone else from homing in on you. And, you have no choice but to accept their help. Your beacon gets brighter and easier to follow the more you develop your power."

Grams floated over to the window and looked outside

before turning back to the group. "We need to get to work. You need more practice with potions and adding Fae runes to them."

"Coffee first, then we can get back to work." I headed for the door, trusting that I wouldn't lose my grams again. There was no way I could continue without a boost. And some food.

CHAPTER 2

"*D*o you think I'm going to need to give Grams back her room? I just got the new mattress. And I created a closet for my stuff." When my stuff finally arrived at Pymm's Pondside, I realized the armoires weren't going to be big enough to store all the clothes I owned. Violet and Aislinn helped me magically create a walk-in closet.

Aislinn set down her cup of coffee and lifted her shoulders. "No idea. Do ghosts sleep? Wait. What are you going to do when your kids visit during the holidays next month?"

"I don't think ghosts sleep or need a room, but that's the least of your worries. You're a *you know what* and have to make sure that stays hidden. But now you have Isidora to help you learn everything you need to know." Violet used air quotes when she 'you know what.'

"That doesn't change the Backside of Forty. We're a team, right? I can't imagine facing the shit with the Queen without you guys. Don't get me wrong. I'm happy to have Grams back, and I look forward to learning from her, but I need you two."

Violet smiled, and Aislinn nudged my shoulder. "Don't forget Bas. You need him, too."

I rolled my eyes but couldn't stop the smile from spreading across my face. "True. He comes in handy during a fight." I'd given up on the idea of dating and thought my 'port' had been closed for good when I lost Tim, but Sebastian changed that.

"Among other things." Violet waggled her eyebrows. The bell over the door jingled, and they all turned that direction to see their favorite gossip, Mae, enter Violet's bookstore.

The thick raised scar along her throat a brutal reminder that something viciously attacked her at some point. The rasp to her voice told you the injury permanently damaged her vocal cords. It had rendered her siren abilities useless, which meant she could no longer survive in the ocean.

I suddenly wondered if escaping my house and my Grams had been a good idea after all. Sure, my dead grandmother had returned to me as a ghost and spent the better part of the day nagging me to master my power so I could wield it against my enemies, but that wasn't so bad, right? After all, Mae had never brought good news when she stopped in before.

Violet turned to the newcomer with a smile on her face. "Afternoon, Mae. What brings you in?"

"You were closed earlier. Zreegy went to Tunsall and Tierny's home, but she was too late. She called in Gardoss." Mae's voice had dropped at the end, and her gaze bounced around the room. It made me want to laugh. Not that the topic required it, but the woman worried about being overheard.

I tapped the side of my cup and considered what she'd said. My heart raced when she said Tunsall's name. Tierney had to be her friend, or maybe a sister. "Who is Tierny and Gardoss?"

Mae leaned closer to me and lowered her voice. "Tierny was Tunsall's sister. And, Gardoss is Bruce's brother and the Fae equivalent of Lance."

My racing heart skipped a beat, and my chest constricted. I rubbed the area absently. "So, he's a cop?"

Aislinn's head bobbed, and she jumped in before Mae could say more. "He investigates crimes that the Constable can't respond to."

"Why is he here?" Violet's voice wavered as she spoke.

Mae lowered her gaze and swiped a finger under her eye. "There's been another death. Tunsall couldn't call Lance when she found her sister, so she called Gardoss. The murders show no sign of stopping. I just hope Gardoss can do something before anyone else is hurt."

Violet gasped, and her hand flew to cover her mouth. Her gaze was worried when it met mine. "We thought it was over."

Aislinn narrowed her eyes and shot Violet a look that said, keep your mouth shut unless you want everyone on your doorstep asking for blood. I appreciated the support. It would be easy for both of them to turn on me and blame me for the recent deaths in town. After all, it was because of me and my bat signal that the murders started. That's what I suspected, anyway. And, I could see Mae going around telling everyone what I was and inciting a riot with the supes out for my blood.

Mae tossed her long gray locks over one shoulder. "It seems our brief reprieve is over. I wish your grandmother were still here. She'd know what to do. I'm off to see if Bruce has any more information." At the door, Mae turned back to me and scrutinized me for several seconds. "You feel different. I can't put my finger on what it is, but something has changed."

I shrugged one shaking shoulder. My poor middle-aged

heart couldn't catch a break. Just when it started to slow, it kicked right back up. I had to be careful. I wasn't twenty anymore. If my inability to run more than a mile was an indication, there was only so much that old muscle could take.

"I'm closer to forty-one today than yesterday. And, I haven't had enough caffeine today."

Mae chuckled. "That must be it. I'm like a rabid beast without my cuppa joe in the mornings. See you all later."

I turned to my closest friends. "We need to find out if it was the Queen. If she's back, we need to know."

"You're right. Let's go to her house and see if we can pick up on anything," Aislinn suggested, then turned to Violet. "We will come back and fill you in after we're done."

"Do you have that invisibility potion we made last week?" That was not what I expected to hear Violet say.

I blinked and shook my head. "I didn't bring it with me. Besides, I'm not sure it's a good idea to take it. Seeing as it didn't blow up, I'm fairly certain I did something wrong."

Aislinn laughed at that. "We'll be fine. If Gross is there, the Queen won't dare stick around."

Another customer walked in, and we took that as our cue. With a wave, I followed Aislinn out the door and headed to my vintage mustang. Vintage was code for rusted and barely running.

Aislinn grabbed my hand and stopped me before I unlocked the door. "We don't need to drive. She lives close enough to walk."

Nodding, I scanned the street. The sun was still out, but I couldn't shake the feeling of being watched. Ever since I stepped out of the shop, my neck prickled with awareness.

Aislinn was several feet down the street by the time I gave up searching for what I couldn't see and hurried to her side. "We will need to stay out of Gadross's way if he's still there. He won't take kindly to us investigating on our own."

I quirked an eyebrow at my friend. "Is there something going on between you and Gross? I sense some deeper animosity."

Aislinn's mouth pursed as if she'd just sucked on a lemon. "That was a long time ago, and it never went beyond a couple of dates. No. That's not quite right. They were more hookups than anything else."

The image of Bruce flashed into my mind, and a laugh burst from my mouth. I couldn't picture the tall, gorgeous woman having sex with a guy not even four-feet tall with a big, bushy beard and coarse attitude. "He doesn't sound too smart if he let you get away. Is this going to be a problem?"

"That's the past. I took a vow never to go there again. We're good."

"Oh, good." The rabbit hole couldn't get much weirder. Thank God I was fluent in weird. "Where are we going?"

Aislinn had led us off the main street and into the woods that dotted the countryside. About ten feet from the road, she veered toward a large evergreen that had smoke billowing out of the back. In front of it, there was a short, stalky man that looked a lot like Bruce.

It had to be Gadross. Only he was slightly taller than his brother. And his hair was a lighter shade of brown, but their golden eyes were identical. Aislinn ducked behind a bush, and I dropped down beside her.

When I peered around the shrub, I didn't see Gadross, only the tree. Specifically, the house in the trunk. I wondered how they hid this from humans. There was no mistaking the neon purple door set in the bottom of the wide box. About three feet above that were a set of windows on each side of the portal at the base.

There was smoke behind the glass, but I could see what

looked like doll furniture in various colors. I had a pink couch and a yellow punk bed for my American doll when I was a kid. The sofa through the window looked the same.

Even the bark at the base was a lighter shade of brown than the rest of the tree. The color differential encompassed the trunk and up about six feet. It even came to an inverted V at the top like the roofline of a regular house.

The branches were far lower on this tree than those surrounding it, as well. That had to be intentional, seeing as it gave some protection to the second set of windows that I hadn't noticed until I tilted my head for a different view.

"Let's go around back," Aislinn whispered.

I nodded and gestured for her to take the lead. I could have made it there, but she knew the way, and regardless of what she said, I'd bet the supernatural cop would go easier on her if he caught us.

My thighs immediately started screaming as we walked while squatting low to the ground. I exercised regularly but hadn't been as consistent as usual. Nor had I kept to my New Year's resolution to add lunges and the like to my routine. My ass needed to be toned up.

I wasn't sporting cottage cheese yet, but it was only a matter of time. Plus, my daughter Emmie told me my ass had fallen and was flattening with as much speed as my breasts were reaching for my belly button. I swear those body parts stuck to their goal like there was a key lime pie in it for them at the end.

A tiny figure ran toward us before we even made it to the other side of the house. "Tunsall?"

Tears brimming in her big green eyes, Tunsall looked at me with a quivering lower lip. "Have you come to help?"

My head bobbed up and down before Aislinn could say anything. "We will do what we can. What happened?"

Tunstall's gaze shifted from me to the back of her house. I

noticed the light brown coloring continued. I couldn't tell if there were windows back here because the tree's entire back was missing. I got a perfect glimpse of the embers and charred furniture.

"My sister and I were attacked an hour ago. Fire shot through the windows, and Tierny tossed me out the window right before a bomb went off. She... she's gone." The tiny brownie started wailing and wrapped her arms around her waist.

Aislinn laid a couple of fingers on one of her shoulders. "Has Gadross discovered anything?"

She sniffled and wiped her eyes with the back of her hand. "I don't know. He hasn't said anything yet."

"Where was your dad when this happened?" I scanned my surroundings but didn't see anyone else. My hearing wasn't sharp enough to pick up on movement in the area around us.

"He hasn't been released. I'm so sorry, Fiona. I sabotaged you for nothing."

Aislinn snorted. "I could have told you she wouldn't let him go. Evil people like that never follow through on their promises."

I wanted to stand up for Tunsall, but I agreed with Aislinn, so I kept my mouth shut. Tunsall stiffened and moved away from Aislinn. "I know you're right, but what would you have done if she was threatening your family? I had no choice."

"There's always a choice. What matters most is whether you can live with your decision and look yourself in the mirror. There is nothing worse than betraying your integrity. You never get a reprieve from the contempt in the mirror or disdain in your mind. You hurt my friends and me, but I understand that you were doing it to save your family. I only hope you learned your lesson in this process because Aislinn is right. You can never trust someone who doesn't value life."

Tunstall's head dropped. "I will make this up to you, I promise."

I waved that away and fell onto my ass. I couldn't keep crouching anymore; my thighs were burning like a sinner in church. "Ouch!" Lifting one cheek, I picked up a dark green oval from beneath me. It was iridescent and more rigid than steel. It glinted when I lifted it above my head.

"Where'd you get that?" Aislinn demanded as she took the object from my hand.

"I sat on it. Why? What is it?"

"It's a dragon scale, but what is it doing out here?" Aislinn's eyes bounced between Tunsall's house and the object in her hand.

I'd read about dragons the other day and recall something about them breathing fire. "Oh my God. A dragon did this? Why would the Queen call in the big dogs when she could use far fewer resources to get rid of Tunsall and her sister?"

"You're right. A dragon couldn't have done this. If one had, it would leave nothing standing," Aislinn explained.

"That makes sense. I don't imagine dragons can customize the size of fireball they spit out of their mouths." I turned to Tunsall. "Did you or your sister piss anyone else off?"

Maybe the Queen hadn't been behind the deaths after all. Perhaps they'd been looking in the wrong place. The Queen used others in her plot to steal my power, but she did the work herself when it came to the nitty-gritty.

I appreciated that work ethic. And understood it. There was nothing like the satisfaction of shocking people and proving what you could do. Particularly when they underestimated you or judged you based on something like your title. Most would think a Queen never got her hands dirty. Just like few doctors saw me as capable of hooking patients up to ECMO when it was usually a doctor's job.

"We keep to ourselves. I don't even know how we got on the Queen's radar at all. I've always thought it was because Isidora trusted us and always allowed free passage through Pymm's Pondside. Now, I have no idea."

"Maybe it was the Queen," I ventured. "This scale could have been planted as a diversion."

"There's one way to test that theory. Do you sense her presence here? After your encounter with her, you should be able to detect remnants of her presence," Aislinn informed me.

Taking a deep breath, I closed my eyes and focused on the elements surrounding me. Initially, the magic well I'd become used to calling upon was a dry lakebed. Within a few seconds, power trickled in and filled my gut.

Without any direction, I focused on the earth, the plants and trees, and then the beings close to me. My finger tingled with each new element. Every element surrounded me, and they added another layer to the magic I carried in my chest.

At first, it was a jumble of feedback in the form of energy and elements. I tried to pick Aislinn out of it all. My skin buzzed when I was able to isolate her signature from everything else. It was easy to pick apart the different threads after that.

I recalled the way the Queen's energy suffocated me and pulled at my insides. I now knew she was trying to steal my battery, for lack of a better description. Thanks to how Grams explained it to me, I would always see a lithium cylinder in my chest, feeding my magic.

Keeping the Queen's signature in mind, I searched the area around us. There wasn't even a hint of her presence. What I did sense was pure evil. It's what I imagined it would be like when looking into the mind of a serial killer.

"It wasn't her. It was something far, far worse than that."

Tunsall was shaking like a leaf, and Aislinn's complexion had lost all color. "What are we looking at now?"

I shook my head and tried to push the heaviness that weighed on me away. "I have no idea, but I have never felt anything so horrible." None of us will survive what it has planned for our town. I kept those thoughts to myself, not wanting to cause mass panic.

CHAPTER 3

*B*y the time I returned home an hour later, I was exhausted and ready for a nap. Whenever chaos started up in my life, it tended to take over. I didn't get enough sleep or enough caffeine. When the two combined, it created the perfect storm, and I struggled to function.

I was seriously beginning to doubt my grandmother's assertion that I had some kind of internal battery. I could barely lift my arm to wave at the seriously sexy Fae glaring at me from across the yard. My heart didn't seem to feel the fatigue as it started racing in my chest. God, he was sexy as hell.

"Hey." It was a weak greeting, but I had nothing more to give at the moment.

"When were you going to tell me Isidora is back, Butter-fly?" The ever-present glower was on Bas's gorgeous face telling me he was annoyed. He couldn't be too mad because he was using the nickname he'd chosen for me recently.

Much like I had from the first time I met him. I fought the urge to apologize. I didn't owe him an explanation. Sure, I was excited to see where this relationship went and was falling for him, but I hadn't had time to process it myself fully. I'd been doing what I needed to do to take care of myself and make sure I didn't get lost in the shuffle when we learned about Tierny's death.

My life didn't, and would never again, revolve around someone else's needs before my own. It was one of the benefits of starting over. I could set the stage from the beginning. And hope my overeager hormones didn't betray me.

I pinned Sebastian with a stare. "Hello, Fiona. How was your day? It looks like potion-making was productive." I cleared my throat and dropped the deep rasp, returning to my normal tone of voice. "It was rather eventful. I'm still processing everything but more worried about the hostility I picked up at Tunsall's house when I went to investigate her sister's murder."

I've learned a thing or two about balance and the importance of self-care. I spent more than half of my life taking care of my kids and my late husband. I lost my footing after Tim died. Thankfully, I had my kids to keep me busy. And just when I faced an empty nest, my grandmother died, and I moved halfway across the globe to another country. I knew you weren't supposed to make significant life decisions at times like that, but it felt right, and I didn't regret it for a second.

Of course, I did wonder if there was something magical driving me here. I'd say the chances are good that Grams had not only cast a spell to tie her spirit to me but had also placed an enchantment on me to want to remain at Pymm's Pondside and take over the family job.

Bas lowered his head and rubbed the back of his neck. "I get it. I was rude." He closed the distance and wrapped his arms around me, then placed a gentle kiss on my lips before pulling away. I wanted his mouth back. Suddenly my fatigue was gone, and my body was gearing up for an altogether different adventure.

"But I was shocked when I returned half an hour ago and found Isidora floating in the kitchen and watching Kairi through the window above the sink. Wait. Someone killed Tierney? What happened?"

I sighed and threaded my fingers with his, then headed inside the house. Grams needed to hear this, as well. "Grams," I called out while I toed off my shoes in the mudroom.

I was entering the kitchen and heading toward the coffee pot when she floated through the ceiling. "What is it? What happened?"

I let go of Sebastian's hand. "Mae came into the bookstore while we were there and informed us there had been another murder, and Gadross is here to investigate. Aislinn and I decided to go to the scene and see if it was the Fae Queen."

"That was dumb. Never search her out without me being with you," Bas cut in.

I turned and glared at him before continuing. I gave them a brief rundown of what we encountered when we arrived, then showed them the scale and my theory that someone planted it to point the investigation in the wrong direction.

"Placing the blame on dragons would further hinder the relationship between them and the main residents in town." Grams translucent figure seemed to vibrate and get faster as she spoke. "That would cause a rift between Fae and shifters, further dividing the supernatural population. I spent years trying to bridge the rift and bring them together."

Sebastian straightened from the island and lifted his hand to reach for Grams but then let it fall to his side. "Without you, they would be openly fighting for no reason. As it stands, we agree we need to work together to ensure humans never learn about us."

I poured myself a cup of coffee and added peppermint creamer. "That would be bad. I will do what I can to help the situation. And that starts with discovering who is responsible for Tierny's death. Whoever is responsible has some seriously evil intentions for our kind. The negative energy was chilling."

Sebastian came over and rubbed a hand down my back, leaving it there to comfort me. "It's likely the Queen. She has to be getting desperate. Especially now that your energy isn't easily detected."

Grams nodded her head which looked eerie when the tree outside was visible through her visage. "That will help keep attention off of you. We can only hope she buys that she was wrong about what you are. After all, the fight you two had wouldn't weaken a nicotisa like it would other hybrids."

Sebastian's eyes flared wide, and his jaw clenched. "You're a nicotine." It was a statement, not a question or clarification. "I should have known, and you should have told me. I could have done more to shield her from discovery. This complicates matters."

Grams folded her arms over her chest while red flickered around the edges of her ghostly form. "Why should I have trusted you? Yes. We have been friends a long time, and no, you have never given me a reason to doubt you, but with your previous connections, I couldn't be sure. And, I will never endanger Fiona's life. It's why I sacrificed a closer relationship with my granddaughter." Tears seemed to brim in her eyes.

I hadn't considered how difficult it was for her when she sent my parents and me away all those years ago. A thought popped into my head and was out of my mouth before I had time to think about it. "If it was so dangerous, why did I come here every summer?"

"How else was I going to renew the spell?"

I shook my head. "I'm sorry I didn't keep coming back. Life got so busy, but if I'd known..." I let that go. I'm not sure what I would have done if I'd known.

"By the time you were thirteen, it was cemented in place. Now, about the Queen and this energy. Are you certain it wasn't her?"

I wasn't quite ready to let the topic drop, but I wasn't sure how much more I needed to know. "Our magic touched, or something, when we fought, and I felt her. There's this angry determination to her that was lacking in the energy today. At Tierny's, there was hatred and hunger. Whoever did it enjoyed killing the brownie and wanted more."

"Perhaps the killer isn't doing it in an attempt to steal the portal from you, after all. We could have been wrong in assuming that was their intention." Bas braced his hands on the counter. His brows furrowed, and his lips pursed. I'd say this was his thinking look, but he wore a resting dick face most of the time.

Heat filled my cheeks when I recalled how Aislinn told me I could ease the crinkle in his forehead. I'd been married for a couple of decades and had three kids, but I was unsure and nervous about taking it to the next level with him. Part of me was beyond the insecurities and worrying about whether or not he'd like my body. While the other screamed to do some sit-ups and get a better moisturizer to hide the wrinkles.

"I don't think it's the same person. This one was far different from the previous ones. Besides, can they use the blood they took from the others for anything else?" I took another sip of my coffee, enjoying the minty flavor. Some people liked pumpkin spice, but I preferred peppermint.

"Not that I'm aware. Isidora, can witches use Fae blood in spells?"

Grams waved a hand through the air, and energy from it

hit me in waves. It tingled everywhere it touched. "Of course, but it's tricky to work with it. One has to collect the blood in a specific ritual, similar to how one does it for Fae rituals. Not many witches are willing to do such dark magic. Everything comes at a cost, and when you perform blood magic, it eats at your soul and will eventually drive you crazy."

I shuddered at the thought. "No, thank you. I could be wrong. The Queen might have killed Tierney. All I know is whoever did this was beyond angry."

"Last I heard, the Queen was enraged. Has that changed?" I gaped at Grams' question. She did have her finger on the pulse of Cottlehill.

"That hasn't changed. It's what prompted her to make a move against Fiona."

One corner of Grams' mouth quirked up. "Well, that and the fact that you're interested in my granddaughter."

Sebastian's face tinged with pink, and he stopped glowering to give his version of a smile. "That would certainly add to it, but this started before I acted on anything."

"He's right, Grams. She was killing people long before he said one word to me. What's the history there?" I recall him telling me they had a relationship, but he never gave me any details.

Sebastian took a deep breath and closed his eyes for a second. "You know she's married to Vodor. Well, she and the King haven't been close for centuries. What you might not know is that Fae are lusty creatures and sex outside a mating is common."

My girl parts sat up and took notice when he mentioned Fae being horny. I wanted to strip him bare and show him how turned on I was. The tone of his voice alone was like an intimate caress. Shit. He was still talking.

Get your head out of the sewer and join him in the gutter.

"The King has had a harem since he came of age, but the

Queen didn't. Not officially anyway. The problem came when she fell in love with someone else. She talked about overthrowing the King with her lover. Somehow word got out to her parents, and they weren't happy. They'd arranged for her to mate with Vodor when he was making a play for the throne. She begged the man she loved to step up, but he refused." Bas's eyes went distant, and I could see him reliving the events as he talked. His body became stiffer and stiffer as time passed.

"Why did he refuse?" Resting dick face was back, and I hated it. I hoped my voice would ground him in the present.

He blinked several times and finally focused on me, but it was Grams that answered me. "Politics. Only those in the upper echelon of Fae society are powerful enough to take the throne. The reason for classes among the Fae goes beyond income. They value power more than anything. That's why the Queen wants to steal yours, Fiona. You could eclipse her status."

"She's right," Bas added. "The man she loved wasn't in the upper class, and despite being powerful enough to grab it, had no desire to. The Queen was pissed when he refused. She's always been a megalomaniac, and even then, she wanted the man most powerful for her mate. This refusal embarrassed her and was a huge scandal. It was unheard of that the Queen wanted someone who was officially from a weaker family than Vodor."

"You're that man, right?" There was no doubt in my mind. He exuded this aura layered with undeniable strength.

Sebastian lifted one shoulder. "I was, but that's not important. We need to focus on the Queen and why she's been so silent."

"It matters more than you know. She hasn't gotten over you. I imagine she feels you snubbed her by rejecting her then taking off. That, coupled with her desire for my power, makes her highly dangerous. And, it could have driven her over the edge. She might now be lashing out without a care for who she hurt."

"That sounds like the most plausible explanation I've heard all night," Grams agreed with a bob of her head. "And, don't forget your manners, Fiona. You haven't offered Bas tea or anything to eat."

I rolled my eyes at my grandmother but couldn't stop the chagrin. She and my mother had taught me better, and I was making them look bad. "I'm not sure about you, but I could use some wine. Would you like some whiskey? I'll throw a pizza in the oven."

"I'll get it." Bas crossed to the cabinet and grabbed the whiskey, then pulled the white wine from the fridge. A smile crossed his face when he retrieved the stemless wine glass from the counter. It said, 'I pair well with wine.'

After preheating the oven, I put a frozen pie with tomatoes, garlic, and basil on a cookie sheet then took a seat at the island. "Are we safe here?" I couldn't shake the feeling that I wasn't capable of beating the Queen. That meant everyone that lived at Pymm's Pondside was in danger. That included my grandmother now, too.

"Your wards are as good as any I've ever cast," Grams told me. She was beaming at me. The pride was unmistakable.

"Thanks, but are they impenetrable? I don't want anyone else in danger because of me."

"I found all of the spelled stones Tunsall planted, so those aren't a problem anymore. And, you've already tightened those permitted to enter."

Grams made a noise that sounded like she was choking. "You've banned anyone from entering Pymm's Pondside?"

I got up and put the pizza in the oven. "Yeah. I had no choice. Those creatures nearly killed Kairi and me because the Queen manipulated Tunsall into doing her dirty work. I had to make sure that couldn't happen again."

"What about those seeking passage through the portal? Did you ever consider how such a spell would affect them? Most of them are running from the tyrant in Eidothea, and you've barred the only safe passage left for them."

I swallowed and turned to face my grandmother. She had her hands on her hips, but I was glad to see she wasn't red around the edges.

"That's why the portal has been silent since my fight with the Queen. I thought it had to do with her for some reason. I had no idea that would happen." I bit off the apology. I had no reason to be sorry. This was all new to me, and I had been doing my best with what I had.

"Of course not. I blame Filarion. If that weasel hadn't come in and stolen my book, you would have seen my letter, and I would have been here to help sooner. What's important now is to loosen the wards."

Sebastian finished the drink he'd poured himself and set the glass down. "Is there something we can do to ensure no one with malicious intentions can cross over?"

Grams floated closer to the oven when I opened it and watched as I removed the pizza. "That's complicated."

"That's what I thought I did before," I interjected. When I cast my wards, I even kept that desire at the front of my mind.

"Magic isn't capable of evaluating a person unless they practice dark magic. That changes a person, as I said a bit ago, and because of that, we can keep those individuals out. But it can't detect what someone is thinking. Or if they are jealous of you. Nor can it tell when you're hungry and provide you a meal. It becomes tricky when dealing with an individual under coercion to do someone else's bidding."

"That makes sense. Do I hope no one else is manipulated like Tunsall?"

Bas shook his head. "That wouldn't be wise. I guarantee she will find someone else to manipulate sooner or later. That's one of her constants. You need to assume it will happen."

I threw my hands up in the air. "Is there anything I can do? She almost killed Kairi last time. I promised her a safe place to live after she ran from Vodor instead of giving him a piece of herself." She knew the worst thing she could do for her people was give him power under the water. I respected that and wanted to make sure she could live as safely as possible, even if she was away from everyone she loved.

Grams floated back to the window. "We can call on Theamise. She and her sisters can keep an eye on the borders and let us know if something seems fishy."

Bas poured another glass of whiskey while I cut the pizza. "Yes. It wouldn't strike anyone as odd if they struck up a conversation with them. A few well-worded questions and she should be able to determine if someone is acting out of character."

I went to the fridge and grabbed the fruit from inside, and put it on the island. "Sounds good to me. I'm going to take something to eat outside and talk to her and Kairi so I can remove the wards. I don't like the idea of Fae being stuck in Eidothea and in danger."

I grabbed a platter and arranged the food before heading outside. Sebastian followed me with our drinks and the pizza. Guilt ate at me for cutting off the one escape route Fae needed. I couldn't imagine if Kairi was still in Eidothea. The King would have caught her and gotten what he wanted, and it would have been my fault. I hoped the weight on my shoulders would lessen now that Grams was with me and could help me figure shit out.

CHAPTER 4

"*S*o, it's been quiet because you accidentally closed the portal?" Violet clinked her margarita glass against mine. We were at Phoenix Feathers, the pub where Aislinn was a bartender. "Good job, Fi."

The first time we came here, Aislinn had spent more time talking to us than serving others. I asked her why she wasn't afraid of being fired, and she'd laughed at that, saying she'd like to see her mom try. Apparently, her family had owned the place for decades.

Anyway, I had spent the past half hour letting them know what happened when I returned home last night. Aislinn chuckled and lifted a glass of soda to us from her perch behind the bar. "That's one way to keep your workload down."

I growled low in my throat. "I wasn't trying to get out of doing my job. I blame Grams. It wouldn't have happened if she'd told me about uh," I cast my glance around, making sure no one was close. It would be my luck to out the existence of supernaturals to humans. "Our family. It's bad enough Kairi suffered for weeks when I had no idea how to do my job. I had to go and do it again because I don't know any better."

Aislinn paused in wiping down the top of the bar. "There's nothing you can do to change what happened before, and you've fixed the problem, right?"

I bobbed my head up and down. "Grams was as hesitant as I was to lower the ward without a way to monitor if anyone crossed onto Pymm's Pondside. It was pretty simple once Bas came up with enlisting Theamise to help if anyone visits. I had no idea she had such an impact on the trees closest to the house. The leaves thinned out, and the bark is peeling now that she moved to the outskirts of my property."

Violet rolled her eyes. "What part of wood nymph didn't you understand?"

I smacked her shoulder while my head did a good impression of a sprinkler, racing back and forth while I checked to see who was listening. "Shush. And, yeah. I get that now. This is all new to me. It never occurred to me before. Hence the reason we're here drinking."

Violet chuckled and took a long sip of her margarita. "And, here I thought we were here so you could avoid your grandmother. You don't seem overly inclined to spend time with her."

"Why is that? You've been whining about not knowing enough about your heritage, and here you have the perfect source right at your fingertips, and you aren't even with her." It was evident that Aislinn was genuinely curious. I shifted on the barstool while taking a drink of my margarita.

Why wasn't I at home talking with Grams? I should be. It's all I've wanted for months, yet I couldn't be there for very long at the moment. As I considered Aislinn's question, I realized a part of me was uncomfortable around her.

I was getting used to magical matters, but this was some next-level shit. To top it off, she said I was different than most others of my kind. It was bad enough that I had so much power it made me a target.

I finished my drink and set the cup on the counter. "Every time I turn around, she has new information for me. A spell cast from across the world killed my parents. In contrast, a fire burned Grams, killing her. She thought maybe it was a dragon but didn't know for sure. Oh, and Emmie will be coming into her powers in the next couple of years, so I have to find a way to tell them what they are."

Aislinn tilted her head. She was the youngest of the three of us at thirty-eight years old. "They'll be fine with it. I bet they even think it's cool."

Violet shook her head. "I'm not so sure about that. They'll be different and need to keep strict control over their emotions, or they will stand out. And, Emmie strikes me as an introvert."

"She hates being in the limelight, but she has a good head on her shoulders, so the control thing should be easy for her. And, it helps that they all live together now. She keeps the twins in line and will make sure there aren't wild parties and whatnot. But she will work herself half to death trying to keep Skylar and Greyson out of trouble. Those two will be a handful, and I can't move back to help."

Aislinn took my glass and washed it out. "You want another one?"

"Yeah. I left Sebastian and my Grams when I left. She was grilling him about his intentions and why I made this glow. I had no idea the amber has never done this before." I held up the charm Bas had made decades ago. He mentioned something about it being for my family or me. I can't recall exactly. I was too busy trying not to ogle the guy while trying to figure out why he hated me at the same time. And then there was the other stuff he made. He had an unreal talent for creating stunning jewelry, weapons, and tools.

Violet reached for the amulet when she stiffened, and her eyes flared wide. Her face went white as a ghost and her face furrowed with terror.

"What is it?" Aislinn and I exclaimed at the same time.

"My kids!" Violet didn't say anything else as she grabbed her cell from her purse. I started biting my thumbnail while Aislinn practically climbed over the bar.

Violet was holding her breath as she removed the phone from her ear and pressed end. She called up the contact for another one of her kids and hit the button. She took a shaky breath, and I switched to chewing my bottom lip while we waited for them to answer.

She was whimpering by the time she ended that call and hit the contact for her ex-husband. "Hey. It's me. Have you heard from Ben and Bailey tonight?"

Tears filled her eyes while she listened to his response. I jumped off my stool and placed a hand on her shoulder. "No. They didn't answer when I called, so I thought I'd check with you. I'm sure it's nothing." Her voice cracked, telling me she was far more worried than she was letting on.

He said something else that had her clenching her jaw. I swear I heard something crack. "There's no reason for you to do anything. I told you I'd keep you posted. I was just checking on them."

She stabbed the end call button while he was still speaking then looked up at me. "The wards I set around the house triggered. They aren't answering."

Aislinn turned to her fellow bartender and told him she would be leaving. I picked up my purse. "That doesn't necessarily mean anything happened, but let's go check to be sure."

Violet nodded and got to her feet. She stumbled and caught herself on the bar. I wrapped an arm around Violet when her legs wobbled with her first step. Aislinn met us at the end of the bar.

I prayed nothing happened to Violet's kids. They were her world. She was one of the best moms I'd ever known. She was always doing small stuff for them. She went out of her way to stock specific proteins for Bailey because she was vegetarian. They had a great relationship.

My heart raced at the same time a vice tightened around my chest as we exited into the cold winter air. Our breath puffed out in white clouds, and I squeezed Violet's shoulder, trying to reassure her and get her to calm down. I was surprised she hadn't passed out yet with how her lungs seemed to stop functioning.

At least that's the way it seemed when I noticed the white cloud in front of her face resembled the scene in horror movies when the next hapless victim was locked in a basement and opened a large freezer. You know the one where the white frost swirls in the air above the freezer right before it clears, and she starts screaming at the sight of frozen body parts.

Okay, not the best image to have at the moment. I wiped it from my mind and clung to the belief they were fine. I wasn't sure the woman that had become my best friend would survive if anything happened to them.

I put Violet in the passenger seat in my Mustang while Aislinn jumped into the backseat. "They're fine. Maybe they're watching a movie and turned off their phones." Aislinn reached through the seats and squeezed Violet's hand.

Violet sniffed, and her body started shaking. "No. Something has happened. I know it in my gut. We have to find them. They have to be okay." Her voice broke at the end, and her shoulders shook with a sob.

Pulling out of the parking spot, I turned onto the street and had to check my speed. My foot refused to ease up on the peddle. I had no idea what I would do if it had been my children. As a mother, my life had been about nurturing and protecting them for half of my life.

The sky darkened, and the air thickened when I turned onto Violet's street two minutes later. "Do you feel that?"

Violet turned tear-filled eyes to me. A check-in my rearview mirror, and I caught the tail end of Aislinn shaking her head side to side. "I don't feel anything. Do you, V?"

"I can't feel anything at the moment. I mean that literally. My body has gone numb," Violet whispered as her gaze remained riveted to her house.

I stopped at the curb, and she was out the door before I turned the engine off. Aislinn and I followed her a second later. "What do you feel?" Aislinn's eyes roamed the neighborhood around us.

The town was small, with more than half of the population being supernatural. It was about ten miles, with the downtown square being the center. Most of the homes closest to the center, with a handful in outlying areas. Violet lived in the middle of town, not far from her bookstore.

Violet paused on the threshold and looked back at us. Her face was the color of a Mike Myers mask, and her blue eyes were bright and filled with worry. It was then that I noticed the front door was slightly ajar.

Aislinn and I ran to catch up with her. My stomach soured, and bile-filled the back of my throat. The open door combined with the oppressive feeling I couldn't shake and Violet's certainty her kids were in trouble had me convinced she was right.

"Violet, wait. Let me go first." I rushed past her before she could tell me no or enter first.

Her house had an open floor plan, and after a short hall opened up into a living room with a connected kitchen. All I saw was some blankets and the throw pillows strewn across the floor. My chest tightened, and I found it harder to breathe. I tried to pick up on any hints of magic cast in the area, but I was too new to that side of my heritage to know if what I sensed was anything or not.

Violet stopped in the middle of the room and bent to pick something up from under the coffee table. I started trembling with her when I noticed Bailey's cell phone in her hand. The teen was never without the thing.

"Bailey! Ben!" Violet called out, but there was no answer.

"I'll check their rooms," I offered and hurried to the second floor and the three bedrooms.

Bailey's room was first. She wasn't there. Her backpack was on the small desk in the corner, but nothing else was out of place. Bailey had neatly made her bed, and her clothes were in her hamper.

I moved onto Ben's room and saw the opposite scene. His dark blue rumpled comforter sat at the end of the bed, and I couldn't see the floor beyond the piles of clothes, shoes, and gaming equipment. I wondered how he managed to find anything in the place. This, too, fit the kid I had come to know.

I peeked into the master bedroom to find it spotless with the bed made. Whatever happened hadn't reached the second floor. I returned to the living room and told Violet and Aislinn as much. "We need to call the Constable and get some help."

Violet bobbed her head and swiped the tears that were now flowing down her cheeks. "I'll call Lance."

"And, I will call Camille and Sebastian. We can cast some locating spells and find them." I wanted to reassure her that they were fine and we would get to them in time, but I didn't. I knew better than to give her false promises.

"We won't stop looking for them until we find them," Aislinn promised.

"Sebastian will be here in five minutes. Camille lives down the street and should be here…"

"Right now." Camille's voice cut me off mid-sentence. "Tell me what happened." I was relieved to see the powerful witch. She and my grams might not get along, but we needed her experience now more than ever.

Violet told her what she knew, which wasn't much. Lance arrived just as she was finishing her explanation, and she had to launch into another recounting of the events. Only this time, Violet left out how she sensed something was wrong with her kids. He wasn't a member of the supernatural community and did not know of our existence.

Lance had called in a unit to collect evidence and told Violet he needed to monitor her calls in case someone called for ransom. It was apparent the kids hadn't left of their own accord, and he fully expected someone to make demands soon.

"Can you think of anyone that would want to hurt you or your kids?" Lance was searching for a place to start an investigation. Unfortunately, there was little forensic evidence left behind. Without a threat, they had nothing to go on. "What about your ex-husband?"

Violet rolled her eyes. "That asshole is too busy starting a new life to worry about the kids or me. He's a cheating jerk but would never do anything like this."

"We have to look at every angle. I'll need his contact information to follow up. If anyone reaches out to you, call me immediately. In the meantime, I want you to download an app to record any calls you might get." Lance continued to provide instructions to Violet.

I exited the house to greet Sebastian when he arrived less than a minute later. "What happened? Whatever it was involved magic and a lot of it."

I cocked my head. Had he experienced what I had? No

one else mentioned feeling anything. "We don't know. I felt this pressure in my chest the second I turned onto the street, and it got much worse when we entered the house, but no one else did. There's a sign of a struggle but nothing really to go on."

Bas pursed his lips and turned to wave to Lance as he walked down the path. The two of us went back inside to find Camille setting up to scry for the kids. She had pulled the kitchen table to the middle of the space and cleared it off.

Knowing what she needed, I went into the kitchen and got a bowl of water plus four candles, then returned as she was pulling herbs and salt along with her athame from the bag she took everywhere. I lit the candles and set them in the four corners, responding to a compass's locations.

With quick efficiency, Camille poured a salt circle around her and stood in the center. She traced the ring, her finger starting in the North before heading to the East, South, and West, then back to North. A blue light flowed from her finger into the perimeter as she progressed. My skin tingled as a wave of energy rippled from Camille outward. It was light and airy.

My mentor stood beside the table and muttered a tracking spell on the children. The water started swirling and clouded over and stayed that way. It didn't show how to find the kids. It was anticlimactic. I hoped we'd have this explosion of fireworks that would light the way to the children.

Switching tactics, Camille cast a reveal spell, and we got a brief glimpse of the kids huddled together in what looked like a dank cave. Violet cried out and jumped toward the bowl of water.

Before I thought my actions through, my legs were in motion, and I caught Violet mid-leap then pulled her off course. We fell to the ground in a tangle of limbs. I got an elbow to my cheek for my efforts, but the last thing we needed at the moment was for the protective circle to burn Violet.

Camille came toward us and cut through the salt, safely dissipating the circle she'd cast. "They're alive for now. And seem to be underground somewhere."

Bas bent down and helped me to my feet. "Let me try." He helped Violet up and hugged her. I'd never seen him so expressive before. He was always so irritable and distant. Seeing this side of him didn't make me think he was a softie at his core, but it did make me fall for him all the more.

After releasing Violet, Sebastian pushed the table back to its original position then swept the salt aside with his foot. He closed his eyes and drew a rune in the air with his finger.

I made a note to ask him about that later. At the moment, I had to catch myself on the back of the sofa when the earth moved beneath me. Light encompassed Bas, and the energy hit me in the middle of my chest like a punch.

Camille's magic was light and tingled, but Sebastian's was like a sucker punch. I did feel energy seeping from around us and traveling to him. Only it was as if it all hit me at once, rather than caressing me like Camille's had.

The light shifted colors before disappearing when he opened his eyes. "They're indeed underground, but something is blocking me from reaching them. That shouldn't be possible."

"Could the Queen have them?" I immediately wanted to call my question back. Violet crumpled when I asked if our vile nemesis could have taken her children.

Sebastian wrapped his arm around me and tugged me to his side. "We can't rule that out, Butterfly." I smiled at his recent nickname for me. I loved that this broody guy showed his sweet side around others. "But I doubt she'd be strong enough to keep up a barrier this strong. Whoever has them will pay. They didn't count on a Fae, a witch, two half-breeds, and a nicotisa coming together."

How the hell had this happened? We'd cast protections on all of our houses. It hit me that I'd loosened them earlier. I never considered they would all be connected. Another tragedy fell at my feet. I was sick and tired of being used by these evil assholes. This had to end. Now.

But first, I needed to find Bailey and Ben. They took priority.

CHAPTER 5

The last twenty-four hours had been one long nightmare. I only wish it had been nothing more than a horrible dream. Unfortunately, it was all too real. Violet's children had been kidnapped and were being held underground.

I had to come home to get Grams' feedback on what we should do next. We kept coming up against roadblocks no matter what we tried. Camille stayed with us, trying to cast various spells until an hour ago. She needed to get a few hours of sleep and eat then she would be back.

Violet was beside herself and hadn't slept or eaten anything since we left the bar the night before. Sebastian stayed with her and Aislinn in case the kidnapper called or showed up. Someone had taken them for leverage.

Parking the car, I jumped out and ran to the back door. I wanted to shower and change, then talk to Grams so I could go back to Violet's house. Energy pulsed around me, and the pinging started up insistently in my head.

I stopped so suddenly that my arms windmilled at my sides, and I nearly fell on my ass. Part of me wanted to ignore the summons. Ben and Bailey were in danger, and time was of the essence.

Guilt immediately raced in to join the party, and a tug of war commenced inside my gut. Shaking my head, I cursed and switched directions toward the family graveyard next to the house. Waiting for my conflicting emotions to duke it out would only waste precious time.

I had a job that I'd inadvertently cut off, and I couldn't ignore it. There could be a Fae in as much danger as Violet's children. From the signals firing in my head, I would guess that's not far off. I'd never experienced it so intensely.

Pushing the crypt door open, I gaped when I saw a guy trying to get through the portal. He must be in imminent danger if he was willing to risk himself. From what I'd read, trying to cross without permission was lethal. Some of the stronger Fae could cast spells, and there was a chance they wouldn't die, but they'd be maimed for sure.

"Can I help you? You need to go through me to get through the portal."

The Fae turned toward me. I cringed when his dark as night eyes leveled me with a murderous glare. "You don't hold power over me. You're weak and insignificant."

I strolled closer to the portal and stopped just shy of the oval hovering in the middle of the room. Light surrounded the area while the scene through the doorway was that of another world. The few times I had been here to deal with requests to cross, the thing wouldn't even appear until I gave the mental command.

"That must sting. That a weak woman like myself will deny your request." No way did I want someone with such horrid views to be anywhere on this side of things.

"I'm going to relish killing you."

I reached up to direct my spell at the doorway between realms. The words never left my mouth. The Fae managed to get an arm and leg through and had grabbed hold of my long hair. He yanked my head, and I fell toward the bright sunshine and vibrant field.

With a shout, I shoved at his hold. Realizing he wasn't going to budge, I kicked his shin and tried to elbow his ribs. They were on the other, and I felt warm air bathing my right arm while the rest of me remained in the cold, damp air of the English countryside. I stumbled back when he released my hair. I'd been trying to evade him.

The wind whipped around me, making it difficult to hear my heart pounding in my ears. The breeze carried the scent of sweet flowers and lush greenery to me, along with rot. I swore the decay must have come from the Fae.

A foreign language spilled from his mouth. I had no idea what he was saying and didn't recognize the dialect. Sparks flew from his fingertips. The electricity from the hand on his side of the passage bounced back toward him. The fragments from the hand that had held my hair were heading right for me.

Jumping to the side to avoid his spell hitting me, I shouted, "*vulnus.*" I was still learning Latin and the words commonly used to cast spells, and that was the only one I could think of to hurt him.

An invisible fist seemed to collide with his head. At least that's what I thought when his skull jerked backward, and blood bloomed on one corner of his mouth.

He snarled and muttered something else right before he lunged for me. The edge of his fingers caught hold of my sleeve. I became his yoyo as he yanked me toward him, and I pulled my body in the opposite direction.

So much for this being a quick side trip.

Curses ping-ponged through my gray matter as I searched for something that I could use to force him to his side again. His shoulder was through now, and his torso was following suit.

He stopped struggling for a second and focused on me. The Fae gave 'creepy stalker' a new name. I prefer finding a Peeping Tom outside my window than have this guy looking at me like that. My body shuddered, and my hair stood on end at the same time I went on high alert.

Sparks flew toward me again, along with a crackle that was louder than the wind. I was more than ready this time and called out, "*clypeus.*" The sparks hit my shield and fizzled to the ground. My victory was short-lived as he muttered a steady stream of words I didn't understand.

A torrent of energy blasts headed toward me, one right after another. My shield dissolved in no time, and I had to duck and roll to avoid the enchantment hitting me. This guy was pissing me off. I danced around and tried to get behind the portal to close the thing.

To my surprise, I couldn't travel past the portal. This thing should bend to my will, dammit! "Whatever sick and twisted plans you have aren't going to happen, asshole. I'm the Guardian, and I told you that you couldn't pass." My growl vibrated through the air, and the portal did a fast shimmy.

The Fae made a choking noise, and more blood dribbled from his mouth. The sight made me smile, but the shimmy stopped, and his body lunged once again. I tried to recall the anger I felt a second ago and direct it to the doorway, but my racing heart and sore body made it difficult to think straight.

Well, that and the fact that I wasn't skilled enough to do this job. Too much had been happening since I moved to Pymm's Pondside. It made it impossible to learn what I needed to know.

For the hundredth time in the past month, regret overwhelmed me. I hadn't stuck with the kickboxing after Tim died. I've always exercised, but I couldn't get into punching and hitting the air while bouncing on my feet.

How long before I wasn't bent over and wheezing like a chain smoker every time I exerted myself? Another energy ball came my way. I leaned backward and instantly regretted it when my back protested. Lowering my hand to the ground, I caught myself right as my abs gave up the fight, and I headed for the floor.

"*Stordire*," I chanted before I pushed to my feet. The Fae gazed at me wide-eyed. I shoved my sweaty hair out of my face and reached for the edge of the portal so I could close the thing. I didn't want to cut him in half, but I wouldn't hesitate.

Something powerful hit me in the center of my chest, knocking the breath out of me. My knees hit the ground hard enough to send pain shooting up my thigh. I'll be lucky if my bad knee ever worked again.

What had Bas told me about fighting the Fae? Something about cutting them off from the elements that fed their power. The problem was I didn't have access to bar him from Faery. Sebastian also said something about Fae not being able to tolerate massive fluctuations in temperature.

"*Caldo*." The spell left my lips and heated the air around me. I conjured wind and sent the heat toward the Fae. Sweat formed on his brow, and he sucked in a breath while keeping his gaze trained on me.

I knew what he was planning on doing. Taking matters into my own hands, I balled up my hands and ran toward him. Before I lost my nerve, I threw my fist toward his face. There was a satisfying grunt when I connected with his cheekbone. It felt like hitting a brick wall.

Wanting to supersize my punch, I muttered a spell to force him back to Faery. I had one satisfying moment where his grunt of pain echoed in my ear, and his lips moved, but no words came out of his mouth.

Everything changed in an instant. He was windmilling his arms while an unseen force pulled him toward the pasture behind him. His long, black hair whipped around his face. I was less than a foot from him, yet I stood there without a problem.

In the manner of a temperamental windstorm, the tornado didn't touch me like it did the Fae. But it did bring foreign scents through the portal to me. Sweet and spicy flowers breezed by me, carrying unmistakable energy with it.

It made my skin flare and burn. Kind of like the last time I had a UTI. There was a tugging in my middle, and I realized it wasn't power that scalded me. That was a million zaps that energized me.

The burn was from the sucking sensation. Something tried to suck my energy from inside my chest. My hand flew to my sternum, and I took a step backward. I didn't want to take my eyes off the Fae. I didn't trust him as far as I could throw him.

He was clinging to the side of the portal. He started to resemble a red bullfrog with big, bulbous eyes. I stopped moving when his arm poked back through the doorway. The air rippled in the middle of his bicep. Telling me the rest of his body was in Faery.

I screamed when his head joined his arm, and his hair fell flat against his face. How the hell was it so smooth and tangle-free? I would look like a dirty rat—way to stay focused, Fi.

No way was he getting through to earth on my watch. Honestly, it was shocking that he hadn't tried to sweet talk me into letting him cross. The warning bells I got when someone had malevolent intentions had been screaming as loud as the wind, but he could have tried.

I didn't have time for this shit. I needed to get back to Violet and continue searching for Ben and Bailey. "Get the hell away from my portal!" I put all of my anger and frustration into my voice. I stood there with my legs braced apart with my fists clenched at my sides.

I fully expected to watch him get pulled into the sky and back to Eidothea. And that was what happened, for the most part. His legs went into the air behind him, but he held onto the edge of the portal. Smoke rose around his hands, and his skin started glowing.

I was going to pry his fingers off the energy, so he was sucked back to his realm. But I never made it to his side. Between one step and the next, I was forced into the air and pulled toward the portal.

I screamed while my body zipped toward the doorway. I needed to force the thing closed. I scanned my mind rapidly and shouted, "*vicino.*"

Between one blink and the next, darkness encompassed me. My hair whipping around my head was the only clue I hadn't passed out. You didn't choke on your hair in dreams. Then there was the whole breathing thing. I couldn't catch my breath.

An unseen force pulled me through some dark tunnel. My heart started racing as a million horrible outcomes popped into my mind at once. God only knew where it dragged me. Either the spell I cast backfired, or the Fae got one in when I wasn't looking. It seemed like I was in that channel for an eternity, but in reality, it probably wasn't long at all.

Suddenly, a light flashed around me, making me blink as I tried to focus. Unfortunately, all I saw were bright spots and the occasional blurry, dark streaks. The only thing I was certain of was that I was still moving through a tunnel. It's what came to mind because I felt more like a sausage in a casing.

My vision never really cleared when the compression around me vanished and dropped me unceremoniously onto a sunny, grassy field—nothing like failing when lives depended on me to succeed.

My lousy knee hit first, and I fell forward, smashing my face into the soft grass. This was bad. Really freaking bad. Where the hell was I? Eidothea? And, more importantly, how do I get back?

CHAPTER 6

*M*y face hurt, and my bad knee was screaming at me. With a groan and more effort than it usually took, I rolled to my back. With a start, I realized I shouldn't be lazing about while my body dealt with aches and pains. A deranged Fae had attacked me.

With surprising speed, I sprang to my feet only to trip over a lump next to me. I glanced down, and my heart skipped several beats when I caught sight of half a body. Green blood flowed from the diagonal cut along the Fae's torso. It was the guy that had been attempting to climb through the portal and attacked me.

I glanced around, looking for the rest of him, and wondered where we were. The bright sun told me I was no longer in Pymm's Pondside. It had been the night before I entered the crypt to deal with the portal.

The question was if I was still on Earth or if I had, in fact, traveled through the portal to Eidothea. More than anything, I wanted to be in California. And, not just because I'd love to go to Disneyland. I could use a visit to the Happiest Place on Earth at the moment.

My heart started racing again, and now my chest clenched around the pounding organ, making it hard for me to breathe. I knew I was naïve with my wishful thinking. I didn't make it a habit to ignore the obvious, but I wasn't ready to deal with the truth.

You have to face reality and find a way to get the hell back home. Violet and the kids need you! Right. No burying my head in the sand. Alright, I steeled my spine and looked at the situation with clear eyes. Even if I couldn't feel the foreign energy surrounding me, the lush greenery surrounding me was proof enough that I was, in fact, in the Fae realm.

It wasn't that the plants appeared all that foreign, either. It was more that they were full and healthy, and their color was far richer. Unlike anything, I'd ever seen on Earth. You're not in Kansas anymore, Toto. Something wet trickled down my cheek as I searched the area for any sign of the portal. I stood in the middle of an open field where there wasn't even a ripple in the air.

Lifting my hand, I touched my cheek and winced. My fingers came away stained red. That's gonna leave a mark. When I hit the ground, I must've cut my face. I lifted the corner of my sweatshirt and dabbed the injury. I was far better off than the asshole that tried to force his way to Earth.

The mere thought of the dead Fae had my gut clenching. That set off a chain reaction in my body that made me shudder and shake while I stood there. Before I knew it, my magic bubbled at my fingertips and singed the cotton of my top when I lost control of it.

It just burst free from my skin and started spraying everywhere like I'd turned on a faucet. To my surprise, it was flowing freely from my chest. I'd never had my power easily accessible in my life. Even after discovering what I was and had tried to grasp it to cast spells. It'd always been a slippery eel and made me work for anything I managed.

To have it literally overflowing from me so readily was unnerving. I waved my hands, trying to dissipate the tingling only to have sparks fly from them. I was a freaking human sparkler. Silver-white streams of energy burst from me in clouds. The air sizzled and popped from them.

I hadn't realized I packed so much of a punch. My Grams' warning that I was a nicotisa echoed through my mind. For the first time since hearing that term, I believed they might be right about me. I had to stop this flow, only I had no idea where to start. The more anxious I got, the bigger the sparks until I screamed when they landed on the grass and burned it.

I stood there and stared at two dozen black marks on the vibrant green ground covering. Bile rose in my throat. I'd even burned holes in the dead Fae. His skin had bubbled and blistered in several spots and was eaten away in others.

Sweat beaded on my brow, and I was shifting from foot to foot as I racked my brain for a way to calm down and stop the flow of my magic. Voices echoed from the forest to my left. Someone must have heard me scream.

I didn't believe every Fae was evil. Still, I had no idea who I could trust and wasn't willing to take the chance that whoever was heading right for me was friendly, so I took off running in the opposite direction.

Trails of smoke followed me, thanks to my sparkling hands. Way to leave a trail of breadcrumbs to follow. If I knew any runes, I'd draw one for cutting off the flow in the air. Kinda like I'd done with sparklers with the kids when they were little.

My chest started burning, but I didn't stop running until I was fifty feet inside the line of trees. No way did I want to run into another Fae. When I stopped and glanced back, expecting to see a trail of smoldering debris.

The smoke was gone. I retraced my steps a few feet, hoping there wasn't a clear trail for them to follow. I managed a deep breath when I didn't see any scorch marks on the ground.

When no voices reached me, I rubbed the sweat from my forehead and tried to make a plan for where to go now. I yanked my hands away from my face, afraid I was going to add burns to the cuts and abrasions, only to find they'd stopped sparking.

I wanted to shout with joy but managed to stifle the urge and settled for a fist pump. The burning sensation on my chest increased, and I reached up and sucked in a breath and let go of my charm.

Blowing on my hand, I stared down at a circular burn on my palm. Using the chain, I lifted the necklace over my head and held it in front of my face. A trickle of blood rolled down my cheek, but I ignored that as I tried to understand what happened to the amber and silver.

A crack ran through the amber that had turned orange around the edges like the thing was on fire. The Celtic knot designs Sebastian had created throughout the silver were still there, but they glowed brightly. As the metal dimmed, I realized the glow the charm always had was gone. It was heavy in my hand and felt heavier.

It was almost as if the thing had died. I choked back a sob. Now was not the time for a breakdown over a piece of jewelry. I had a special connection to the necklace and seeing it damaged broke my heart. Bas admitted he'd created it with his perfect mate in mind. At some point, I started believing that was me.

Delusional much? You barely know him, and you haven't even slept with him yet!

Suddenly my chest constricted, and my vision wavered. It wasn't as if Bas couldn't fix it, but I had come to think of this as a symbol for my new beginning. And, it represented my new life with Sebastian. I had to be losing my mind to be standing in some foreign realm mourning the loss of something I never even had.

Okay, so something definitely happened between the two of us. Sebastian was possessive and protective of me at the same time. Most couldn't read him, but I knew he cared for me deeply. And, it wasn't just because I inherited the Guardianship.

I'd been keeping him at a distance because I need to figure out myself before bringing a new guy fully into my life. I believed there would be time for us eventually. Seeing this made me think I'd lost my chance in my focus on myself.

I had no idea exactly what this meant or why it happened, but I filed it away for consideration when I was safe. Right now, I needed to find shelter and a safe place to hide. Or you could locate the portal and go back home.

I wanted to smack myself upside the head. So much had happened that I'd overlooked the obvious solution. Deciding the best place to search for the way home was the clearing, I headed in that direction.

My heart hammered in my chest, and I jumped every time I heard a noise. So far, I hadn't heard anything other than what I'd expect to in a forest. I was about five feet from the tree line when something small scurried down from the canopy.

Startled, I gasped and clutched my chest when my heart tried to leap out. Part of me couldn't help but notice the lack of energy in the charm while the rest of me was smiling from ear to ear at the cute little lizard sitting on a branch not far from where I was hiding. It reminded me of a leopard gecko with all the colors, except this one had bulbous eyes and was ten times bigger.

Noise from the clearing nearby must have scared it because it jumped, ran across the tree's bark, and disappeared into the canopy. I turned and scanned the area. Not seeing anything, I snuck out from behind the trunk and tiptoed to a massive pine closer to the edge of the forest.

Using the tree to hide me, I poked my head out and scanned the clearing. Three Fae were standing around the corpse. They had on green leather vests with leather cuffs wrapped around their biceps. The cuffs were embroidered with an intricate design in red. Their pants also looked like they were made from hides, only they were darker green and fitted tight to their legs.

They each had a bow stung across their shoulder with a quiver of arrows over one side. Two had long hair with the front braided out of their eyes and gave me a perfect view of their pointed ears, while the third had short hair that was long on the top and falling over his forehead.

They had to be some of the evil King's soldiers. And they were checking out the dead Fae. I covered my mouth with my hand and took shallow breaths. The last thing I needed was for them to hear me as I whimpered and fought the urge to run.

I needed to get home. Ben and Bailey were missing, and a sadistic killer was hunting innocent Fae. I came through the portal here, so it made sense that this was where I would find it to return home.

Lowering myself to the ground, I used the tall shrubs to help hide my location. I scanned the entire clearing, looking for any indication the passage was there. There had to be something like a shimmer in the air.

One of the Fae said something in that foreign language I didn't understand. Whatever he murmured sent my magic tingling and bubbling up from my chest. I shook my palms when they started itching, and sparks flew from my fingertips. Not now.

My pleas seemed to go unanswered, so I forced myself to take deep breaths and slow my racing heart. If I didn't get this shit to stop, I would be discovered, and God only knew what would happen then.

Dark green light surrounded the dead Fae. Two of the Fae there turned the body while the third scanned the tree line. Instinctively, I ducked while whispering a spell to hide me. It was the first time my magic reacted without me prompting it. I felt the power coursing through me. For a split second, the sparks were back.

Fear kicked in when his head shifted my way, and the magic in my hands vanished before it was seen. I flattened myself on the ground and watched the Fae from there. Few looked up or down when searching for danger, so I hoped my position provided enough cover.

The one that was scanning the trees shifted positions and bent to the ground a couple feet from the body. He called out to his cohorts and pointed at something on the grass. I couldn't see anything from my position, but I was guessing it couldn't be good.

For a second, I wondered if it was the portal. Like I said, not many looked up or down. Unwilling to risk being seen, I closed my eyes and opened my senses. Surely I would recognize the elements of home if they were present.

Something tickled my senses, but it disappeared before I could grasp if it was the portal or not. The energy from Earth was there. I was sure of it, but I couldn't quite grab hold of it. As the Guardian, I should be connected to the damn thing. I couldn't stay here in Eidothea. Violet and Ben, and Bailey needed me. So did Grams and Sebastian.

The ground beneath me vibrated, making me squeak in

surprise. Something big was approaching. My mind immediately conjured images of a T-Rex stomping chasing a Jeep. Please don't let there be man-eating beasts here.

The three in the clearing straightened from their crouch, and all stood together facing the same direction. It was then that I caught sight of a dirt path in the trees on that side. The vegetation wasn't as thick in that direction which was why I didn't head there, to begin with, but I hadn't seen the road.

Dust preceded at least twenty men on horses. Only these were not normal horses. Their eyes were dark red, and their hair was various shades from white to black and everything in between. They also seemed to be foaming at the mouth. It could be that they'd been run hard, but I somehow doubted that. They exuded danger and aggression.

The most significant trait was the fact that they stood six or seven feet tall. Of course, it could be my vantage point that skewed my opinion. The new arrivals with their snarling beasts made every cell in my body scream for me to get up and take off into the woods. I was toast if they found me lying there.

You got this, Fi. Just stay hidden for now.

I was glad my inner badass was confident because I was literally shaking in my boots. And, my back was screaming at me, making it next to impossible to stay still much longer. I didn't think this through, and I should have before plastering myself to the ground. I knew better than to put my creaky joints to the test like this.

The leader of the new arrivals jumped from his horse next to the body. "Do we know who this is?"

One of the original Fae shook his head side to side. "No, sir. I can't get an identity, but there is something you should see."

The leader's eyes narrowed. "What's that?"

The Fae that had spotted something a couple feet from

the body pointed to whatever he found. "There's the blood of a hybrid here."

Everyone in the group turned and looked at him, including the leader. "A hybrid? Is it the one the Queen was after?"

The guy that pointed out my blood lowered his head, and I could see his throat work when he swallowed. "I can't tell. Initially, it seemed as if it held the power that she seeks for King Vodor, but then it was gone, so…I can't be sure of what I saw."

"Spread out. Find the hybrid. Don't return to Midshield without her in tow." The leader took two steps, then launched himself into the air and landed on the back of his horse.

The soldiers started talking and shifting, and I took advantage of the momentary chaos. I wasn't going to stand around and wait to be discovered. I might as well jump out and give myself up.

I ran for several feet before I realized I was making a crap ton of noise. Veering to the right, I changed directions and slowed to a walk. My muscles jumped, and I bounced with each step, but I refused to allow myself to run again.

Sweat trickled from my brow as I made my way through the area. Wiping it with the back of my hand, I noticed it wasn't sweet at all but was blood. Crap. Stopping in my tracks, I glanced back to make sure I didn't leave a trail behind me.

I caught red on some leaves and cursed under my breath. Can't leave those breadcrumbs to be found. "*Collectum sanguinis*," I muttered. Energy trickled from me and floated along the path I'd just run.

Please work, please work. A second later, the drops of red floated toward me and pooled in a circle in front of me. That needed to be buried deep beneath the soil. I wasn't sure where that came from, but I learned to trust my instincts, so I grabbed a broken branch and started digging.

When I reached four feet down, I stopped and wondered how I would get it into the hole. I tried to grab hold, but it wouldn't budge. Next, I sprinkled dirt over the top of the sphere—still nothing.

Hands-on my hips, I stared at it and tried to estimate how far to the bottom. It was at least eight feet, and it wasn't moving. "'C'mon. Get in the freaking ground already." I blew my breath through my lips, making a 'phbt' noise. A second later, the blood glowed and dropped into the grave I'd dug.

"Thank you, sweet baby, Jesus," I whispered and pushed the pile of dirt back on top of the buried blood.

After adding the biggest rock that I could lift to the dirt on top, I took off again. My heart clenched the farther I got from the portal and my ability to return home. My mind went to Ben and Bailey.

"I will find you," I vowed. Energy sizzled throughout my body as I raced through the trees and shrubs, searching for a place to hide so I could regroup and get home.

CHAPTER 7

After what felt like forever running, I stopped and leaned against a tree. I was a sweaty mess, my legs were cramping, my bad knee was threatening to give out entirely, and I could barely breathe.

When I tilted my head back to gauge the sun, something grabbed hold of my hair. I yelped and jumped at the same time I tried to turn around. My heart raced so fast it made me dizzy. Or it could have been my attempt at Tae Kwon Do. I had never been all that athletic. The only thing missing when I ran was a massive hump on my back. I was the spitting image of Quasimodo, the Hunchback of Notre Dame. Only I likely embarrassed him.

Clutching my chest, I scanned the area for a soldier, certain I had been followed and was stupid to let my guard down. There was nothing but trees surrounding me. It wasn't until I lowered my gaze to check the ground that movement caught my eye.

A sigh left me when I saw a woman that looked like Theamise. "You scared the crap out of me." Her stick-like arms shook along with the rest of her body.

I held up my hands. "It's okay. I won't harm you. You're a wood nymph, right? Do you know Theamise? That's a stupid question. She lives at Pymm's Pondside with me."

"Thea? She's well?" Her body stopped quaking, and she stood up straight. She was just as tall and thin as Theamise. She had pretty green eyes, too, and a wide smile.

My head bobbed up and down as my heart slowed. I was no longer wondering if I'd suddenly developed vasovagal syncope, but I still couldn't quite catch my breath. "She's wonderful. Keeps my trees healthy all year round, despite the cold weather during winter. I'm Fiona. What's your name?"

She stared at the hand I held out to her then lifted her gaze. "I'm Danalise. Are you the hybrid the King is searching for?"

"What do you know about that?" My gut twisted into a knot.

"His guard is roaming the countryside searching for you. He wants to get his hands on you before Queen Thelvienne does. She's after your power isn't, she?"

My jaw dropped, and I wondered if Danalise was someone I could trust after all. Just because she looked and sounded like Theamise didn't mean she was. "I'm not sure why she would want anything from me. I'm nothing more than a weak hybrid."

Danalise closed some of the distance between us while twisting her hands together. "You're anything but weak. You can't let them capture you. The King will do far worse than the Queen. This realm will not survive if they gain any more power. Many families are already gone."

"They've moved to Earth?"

Her head shook back and forth. "Some fled the realm, but most didn't get the chance. They were killed. There are so few of the upper-class families left anymore."

"The Queen is killing them? For their power?" I disliked this realm more and more every second.

"King Vodor is the one that has been systematically gathering families and taking them to the dungeons. Of course, he doesn't admit to draining them. False charges are brought against them, and they are never heard from again. Within days everyone across the realm feels the drain."

"Because you're each connected to the realm and its health." I recalled reading something in Grams' grimoire about the intimate connection between the realm and its inhabitants. "Why would he do something that would threaten his planet? He'd eventually be King of nothing."

Danalise laughed, and the sound was more like leaves rustling in the wind. It had to be the oddest noise I'd ever heard from anyone. "He's insane. He got his position by stealing power, and he can't maintain it without consuming as many Fae as he can. It's made him unstoppable. We've lost hope that there will ever be anyone to set us free. Especially when the Queen is following in his footsteps."

I clenched my fists and channeled my anger into my determination. "I won't let that happen. I have to return home, but I will not stand by while your realm is destroyed little by little."

Danalise's lower lip quivered, and her eyes filled with tears that never fell. "You're the one the elders have been whispering about."

"Ummm," I drew out as I tried to stop the panic before it bubbled over and out of control. Just because I would do everything in my power to ensure they weren't killed didn't mean I wanted the weight of their world on my shoulders. That was too freakin much pressure. It was all about rest and relaxation in my new life.

That was the plan when I decided to leave my job at the hospital and move to England. I'd had a lifetime of lives hanging in the balance with me being key to their survival. I was done with that. Wasn't I?

"I'm not so sure about being that person, but I promise I will help make sure your situation here is better. But first I need to get back home. My friend's children are missing. I think the Queen kidnapped them. Can you tell me where I am?"

She tilted her head and stared at me. "You're close to Cragpost."

Well, that didn't help me at all. "Right. Cragpost. But where is that? Is that where the King lives?"

Danalise grabbed my hand and tugged me to our left. "He lives near Midshield. Cragpost is a small town. Most that live there are brownies, but there are dragons, Fae, and some ogres, as well."

"You said I was being hunted. How does anyone know I'm even here?"

She chuckled. I thought so anyway. Her shoulders shook gently, and I heard leaves rustling in the breeze again, only this time it was faint. "Like you said. We're all connected to Gaia here. You sent out ripples of energy when you came through the portal. Our kind will be flocking to the clearing in the next day to try and catch a glimpse of you."

I gasped as my hand flew to my mouth. "I won't be able to get through if the clearing is being watched and I have to get home. Children are counting on me. And other supernaturals too. The Queen is killing our kind back on Earth."

"The Queen? How is she killing when she's been here for seven or more months and hasn't left?"

I stopped walking, and because Danalise was still holding my arm, she was jerked to a halt, too. "How can that be? I fought her myself not that long ago. I haven't even been the Guardian that long."

Danalise smiled wide, showing off her straight white

teeth, and let go of my arm. "That's why she was burned over three-quarters of her body and hasn't left the castle since she returned. I knew you were the one. Although, her return tipped the King off to your existence."

Shaking my head, I stifled the urge to scream. She hadn't heard a word I said. I wasn't there many months ago, and there was no way Grams had been in a position to battle a Fae as powerful as the Queen. "That could not have been me. I didn't live in Cottlehill Wilds until a few months ago. Grams was still alive seven months ago."

"Oh! It's hard to remember you know nothing about our realm. You're powerful and feel like one of us. Time moves differently here than where you're from. How much it differs fluctuates depending on the time of the year, but times passes faster here compared to Earth."

I bobbed my head and started walking again. "So we're near a town. Is it safe for me to be there?"

"Yes! 'C'mon. I have someone I want you to meet." She was dancing out from between the trees and crossing a dirt road in no time.

I hurried to catch up. My feet stopped at the edge of the forest, and I looked both ways. I felt like a kid again. When I was five years old, I was terrified of crossing a street because my mom warned me about how dangerous cars were. It wasn't vehicles that had me frightened at the moment. I had no desire to be caught by those soldiers.

I raced across to where Danalise had paused to wait for me. The trees weren't as thick here, and I felt far too exposed. The wood nymph talked about us being just in time for dinner. I barely heard what she was saying.

I was too busy taking in what I assumed was Cragpost. There were small rounded huts, toadstools with doors and windows, and trees made into homes like Tunstall's. There were also large homes made of stone. Several had thatched roofs. Others were similar to the stone shingles made to resemble a straw roof on my house at Pymm's Pondside.

"Where exactly are you taking me?"

Danalise pointed to the most prominent building in the area. It was made of dark blue stones. "To see Argies. He's the leader of the Insurrection. He'll want to meet you."

"Does he lead something like a rebellion against the King?" I asked as she paused in front of the black front door.

The panel swung open, and the tallest guy I'd ever seen stood there glowering at me with blue eyes and messy brown hair. "That's precisely what it means." His voice was a menacing growl, and it caused shivers to race up and down my spine. "Who have you brought Danalise?"

"This is Fiona. She's the one that will help remove the tyranny and save us all."

I grabbed Danalise's arm and cleared my throat to stop her from making promises about me I wasn't sure I could live up to. "I'm not so sure about all that, but I will help in any way I can. After I return to Earth and help save Ben and Bailey."

Argies held his door open with one hand and gestured inside with the other. "You'd better get in here. You never know who's listening in."

I scanned the area, not seeing anything. "There's no one here."

He grabbed my arm and yanked me into his house. Were all the sexy Fae broody assholes? Danalise walked through next, and the door slammed after her.

His scowl lessened, and he became even more handsome. "Watch yourself. The King has spies everywhere. The last thing any of us wants is for you to be discovered. Dana wouldn't say anything unless she was certain you were the one."

I couldn't help but roll my eyes at that. I hated the idea of a prophecy that one individual was going to save the world. There wasn't a being alive that could do it alone. "I'm not the subject of some prophecy, so you can continue your search."

Argies stalked down a hall that was paved with stone tiles in light greys. We passed a room that looked like a family room with sofas, a chair, and a low table. The walls were golden brown, and the wood furniture matched. The furniture looked like it was covered in leather with plush cushions.

On the other side of the hall was what looked like a library. Three of the walls had floor-to-ceiling bookshelves, but only one set had any books. The rest were filled with treasures of all kinds. I'd never seen anything like it outside the Pirates of the Caribbean ride at Disneyland. I loved shiny gold and jewels, but books talked to my soul. Thus, the reason I had to fight the urge to run inside, grab a book and take it to the family room so I could relax in front of the fireplace.

I tugged Danalise's tight brown top. "He's a dragon?" I whispered when she looked back.

"Yes, I am," Argies called out over his shoulder. I jumped out of my skin and clasped my chest. He was nearly as bad as Sebastian. I wondered if they were friends.

"You don't look like a dragon," I pointed out.

He ignored me as he pushed open some double doors at the end of the hall. We'd passed a set of stairs that lead to the second floor, but my mind was racing with a million questions.

"Seriously though, I'm not your savior. I'm a middle-aged widow trying to start my life over. I have a bum knee and the odd chin hair."

Argies stopped in the middle of a small kitchen and turned his glare on me. It made me want to shrink against the tall cabinets behind me. "No, you aren't a savior. Nor are you the subject of a prophecy. There are no such things. But we do have seers that gave us hope in the form of a powerful hybrid."

I pointed to my chest. "I'm that hybrid." I'd taken everything with a grain of salt so far, but the thought of a being that could see the future was too far down the rabbit hole for me.

It wasn't that the room was small, just that Argies was so big he took up all the space. The kitchen made me think of how things used to be before electricity. There was an open brick oven along with what looked like tables. There was a small table with chairs, as well.

Argies went to a dark closet and started pulling out platters of food. "Unless there are more like you in your realm, I believe Danalise is right, and you are that hybrid. Now that we're in a closed environment, I can feel your power."

Danalise lifted the lid off what looked like fruit. Some looked familiar, but it didn't smell like I expected. "She fought Thelvienne. She's the reason the Queen has been locked inside her rooms for months."

One of Argies's eyebrows lifted, and his brow puckered. "Are you sure you're not our savior? I've never seen one of the royal family injured like that."

I waved my hand in dismissal and popped a piece of what I thought was an apple. The flesh was white, and the skin was bright red. My jaw masticated three times before I spat it out and started choking. "What the hell is that?"

"That's dewberries. You don't like it?" Danalise had a frown on her face, and she was looking at me sideways.

"They taste like flowers and dirt. Not my favorite." My mouth felt like a moldy flowerpot.

A knock sounded from the back of the house. Argies left the kitchen in the opposite direction from which we'd entered.

Three tall elves entered, one carrying a plate with what looked like sliced bread. "Marikhoth, Respen, and Eirina this is Fiona. She's the hybrid."

Eirina put the plate down and came at me with her arms out and a smile on her face. Another round of me denying the fact that I was their savior. My heart raced ever faster as these newcomers were excited that I was there to save them.

"We need to organize everyone and come up with a plan of attack," Marikhoth said excitedly as he nibbled on the bread. "Once we know the details, we can have the gnomes spread the word to the other towns, so we have a unified front."

To my surprise, Argies corrected them before I opened my mouth. "That's not happening anytime soon. Fiona isn't staying. She must return to her realm. She has friends in danger. Two of them are kids. It seems someone is terrorizing her town."

Respen gasped and covered his mouth with his hand. "You don't think Vodor sent a *bilge* do you?"

Argies pursed his lips and tapped the countertop. "I'd say it's likely."

I lifted a hand. "Do they have scales and fire? A brownie was killed by fire, and I found a red scale near her house." My mouth still tasted like a hundred-year-old garden, so I grabbed a piece of bread and popped it into my mouth. It was dense and surprisingly sweet.

"No scales. They're black with smooth skin and no fur. They look like a Grimm, a giant dog. And, I'd say it's likely it was trying to hide its actions and set up a dragon." He paused and clenched his hands into fists before continuing.

"We're known to be volatile, and of course, fire is our natural weapon if you don't count our teeth. But no dragon would bother killing a brownie-like that. They're no threat to us. It'd be like burning your snack because it pissed you off. Pointless." Argies broke off some bread and popped it into his mouth.

"Okay, so I'm looking for a black dog. Can you help me get back to the clearing and through the portal? I have to get back home."

Argies shook his head from side to side. "None of us could help you. We'd only bring attention to you, which is the opposite of what you need right now. But you don't want to leave anytime soon. It's dark out, and kobolds are out hunting now."

"We might as well make some plans while we're trapped here. That way, we can gather any supplies and weapons we'll need for when she returns," Marikhoth suggested.

The group started talking over each other, and I sank into one of the chairs at the table and cradled my head in my hands. I was hungry and exhausted and wanted to go home. The second it was safe, I was out of here. I hated the idea of leaving this group in the lurch, but I had no choice.

CHAPTER 8

*M*y hand flew to my hip as a gasp left my lips. My back hurt like a bitch after spending the night on the sofa in Argies's house. You didn't have to lay there being miserable. You were offered a soft bed. The reminder was unwelcome. As if I really had a choice. I was in a foreign realm and had no idea who I could trust. Argies was good-looking, and his group talked a good talk, but I wasn't willing to put my life on the line by letting down my guard.

They were desperate to remove Vodor from the throne. People in that position would do almost anything to achieve their goals. After all, living under tyranny made it, so there was little left to lose. That had me pacing the living room for a while before deciding to try and get some rest.

The sofa was soft but not comfortable to lie on. After tossing and turning and trying to squirm into a better position, I gave up and returned to sitting. At first, it had been fantastic after a long stressful day of running through the woods, but then my back and hips started aching.

I sat there thinking about everything that had happened

and recalling everything I had read about the portal. It felt like hours passed, and it should be morning, but I had no idea how long it had actually been. Apparently, time moved differently in Eidothea than on Earth.

Exhaustion dragged at me, thanks to my inability to sleep a wink. How could I when my best friend's children were missing? Getting back home wasn't going to be a simple task, and Eidothea wasn't a friendly place for me at the moment. I was subject numero uno on the King's wanted list.

I'd already been aware of how awful he was, but I'd learned so much more about how he was stealing the vitality from the Fae to feed his need for more power. Because of that, there wasn't anyone strong enough to battle him for the throne.

This group was staging a rebellion and gathering influential people to overcome the King's power and oust him. They wanted me to help them. I couldn't help but question everything they'd told me. Was it really that unsafe to return to the portal? Were they waiting there for me?

My gut said yes, they were, and I didn't care. I had to try. I wouldn't stay here while Violet needed me. While Argies seemed to support me returning home, I couldn't be sure. I didn't know him and wasn't going to blindly trust him when I knew he needed something from me.

Getting to my feet, I crossed to the window and noticed it was still night outside. There wasn't even a hint of it shifting to daylight anytime soon. I needed to take my chances out there and make my way back.

My stomach rumbled, and fatigue dragged at me, making me hesitate. I needed to eat, and I needed caffeine. Did they even have the nectar of the Gods here? I could always wait around and ask when Argies or one of the others got up. They'd be happy to feed you while outlining all the reasons you can't leave!

It wasn't that I was cold-hearted and immune to their plight. I hated what they were being put through at the hands of some evil megalomaniac, and I wanted to help them. But I had to get home. There was just as much at stake on Earth. More for Ben, Bailey, and Violet.

Glancing around, I searched for something I could grab to eat. I hadn't been brave enough to try very much last night. Who could blame me? The two types of fruit I'd eaten had tasted like mold, and I refused to try anymore. My stomach had threatened to bring it all backup. The last thing I wanted to do was get food poisoning when I was in a foreign place and being hunted by thousands of soldiers.

The bread! While it had been dense and bland, it wasn't awful and would be nice right about now. I hadn't eaten in at least a day, and I wasn't going to make it very far without something.

Opening the cupboard, I saw the plate of biscuits and grabbed three. I had no way of carrying them, so I put one back and searched for a bottle I could fill with water. Stealing from Argies after he'd given me a safe place to rest and food went against every fiber of my being, but I was in a bind.

"Morning." I jumped at the sound of Argies's deep voice. "I didn't mean to startle you."

I clutched my chest and turned around to face the sexy dragon. He was as muscled as Sebastian and nearly as attractive, but he didn't get my motor revving like Bas did. So much for sneaking out. "It's alright. I'm on edge."

Argies crossed the room, and it was then that I noticed the soft pants he was wearing. Alright, so I didn't exactly catch the pants until I forced my gaze away from his chest. Yep, he was sexier than a man who could turn into a giant lizard should be. And, he wasn't malicious like I had begun to think of his kind.

"Did you get any sleep?"

I shook my head to clear the inappropriate thoughts. "Not really. You wouldn't happen to have any coffee, would you?"

He paused with his hand on an upper cabinet. "Coffee hasn't really caught on here. Neither has a television. Two of the reasons I visit your realm as often as I do."

I tilted my head to the side. "I'm a demon without my coffee in the mornings, so you'll want to keep your distance." I hadn't considered the amenities they didn't have here. I scanned the room quickly and noticed something important. "Do you even have electricity here? I know you have toilets like they used to have on Earth about seventy-five years ago but hadn't really considered anything else."

Argies chuckled as he opened the cabinet and grabbed two mugs and a jar. "You've been worried about your friend and her kids since you arrived. I'm not surprised you didn't notice much. But to answer your question, no, we don't have electricity. The magic here interferes with it, so we gave up more than a hundred years ago. You're hungry, I see. That's a good sign."

I jolted at his observation and glanced down at the bread in my hand. I'd crumpled it and held pieces now. "Uh, I am actually. Honestly, I'm not really sure about eating anything. That fruit I tasted last night was awful."

"I understand that. Your food is so different. There's a strong chemical component in your fruits and vegetables. But you haven't tried fried orc. I think you'll like it." He went to the cold storage where he kept food and grabbed one of the plates I'd seen last night. After the fruit, I hadn't looked too closely at anything else, afraid I might see eyeballs or intestines. My mind immediately conjured the creatures from the Lord of the Rings movies, making it even less appealing.

I scrutinized the fried orc and noted it kinda looked like month-old chicken fingers if I squinted and tilted my head just so. "Nope. Baby poop green isn't an appetizing color." My hand covered my stomach as it started to churn.

Removing the plastic wrap, Argies turned a scowl my way. "I didn't say to eat it raw." With that announcement, he selected several pieces and crossed to the brick oven set into one of the walls.

Heat filled the kitchen a second later when he opened his mouth and blew a stream of fire at the slices that he'd carefully set across the stone platform on the grates. My arm shot up to shield my face from the warmth, as well as the bright orange flames.

A mouthwatering aroma filled the kitchen. It leaned heavily toward garlic with sage and thyme added in to make it savory. Reminds me of turkey on Thanksgiving. "It smells delicious, but if it's still baby poop green, there's no way I will be able to eat it."

Argies made a sound, and his flames flickered before they went out altogether. "You're something else, Fiona. Do you trust me?"

I watched amusement dancing in his dark eyes, but I barely registered his teasing. My mind had traveled back to my struggles a couple hours earlier. "I don't even know you," I told him, sharing the conclusion I'd come to. "I'd like to say yes, absolutely, but I know better. Let me ask you something. Will you keep your promise to help me reach the portal?"

Fate must be at work because if I'd left when I wanted and avoided Argies altogether, I would be running around the Fae countryside lost and alone. I had no idea which direction to head.

"I made a promise and will follow through on it, but we need to be careful as we travel to the clearing. It won't do any good if we take the direct route and get caught. The journey will be long and arduous."

My mouth fell open. "What? It took me a day to get here.

Why can't I get back before nightfall? I need to get home." My heart started racing, and my breaths turned choppy.

Argies reached into the oven and pulled out a piece of orc. Instead of the green, slimy strip I expected, he held onto a crispy piece of kiwi. Not the worst. Holding it out to me, he smiled. The look was full of challenge.

"They have all main roads covered, and Vodor has extended the search well into the forest."

I didn't bother overthinking what he was offering. If he was right, I needed to keep up my energy, so I took the meat and took a bite. To my surprise, my teeth sank through the tender flesh, and it was easy to take a chunk of it. Flavor exploded across my tongue.

My eyes widened at how yummy it was. There was a slightly slimy texture, but the flavor overrode that enough that I could swallow. I might be able to eat a couple more pieces, but not much more than that.

"It's alright. The texture takes some getting used to, but it doesn't taste like boiled assholes, which I had expected."

"Have some more. You're going to need your energy. Would you like some tea?"

Shaking my head, I grabbed another piece and wolfed it. "I'll pass on the tea. Get dressed so we can head out."

Argies watched me closely. I ate another piece and was happy it got better the more I consumed. His stare was unnerving and had me fighting the urge to check my hair and face. I hadn't washed the makeup off my face the night before. It never occurred to me.

Thankfully, I was no longer a twenty-something-year-old, or I would be breaking out by now—another benefit of being middle-aged.

I opened my mouth to ask if he changed his mind when he turned and left the room. Picking up one of the mugs, I went to the sink and was happy to find a faucet with a lever to turn the water on and off. I filled the cup and swigged it to wash out the aftertaste.

Argies was back in no time and had grabbed all the remaining orc, some bread, and a few starfruits. At least that's what it looked like to me. It had yellow skin and had a five-point shape to it. He picked up a leather backpack and tossed everything inside.

"Stay close to me. If we get separated, go to the nearest town and search for the flame rune on a building and ask for me. They'll get word to me and keep you safe."

I bobbed my head and followed him outside, only to stop in place. "I have no idea what the flame rune looks like."

He gave me a how-the-fuck-have-you-survived-this-long look, then bent down and drew in the dirt with his finger. "You'll see an orange glow around the symbol, as well. It's hard to miss."

I stared at it for a second then we both stood up. "Thanks. Next time I come back, I will have more knowledge. My Grams recently returned to me as a ghost, and she knows everything and will teach me."

I followed him through his backyard and into the trees. We'd come in the opposite direction, so it was difficult to continue walking away. I'd give him an hour before grilling him about where we were headed.

Traveling with Argies was very different than with Danalise. She and I had run like a bat out of hell to get away from the patrols. Now it was as if I was on a Sunday stroll. Or a date. I wanted to choke myself for the stupid thought. That was the last thing on my mind. But it felt more intimate than I anticipated. My heart was back to hammering while my mind ran through ways to escape him and find my way back to the portal.

I'd follow the ley lines, but I wasn't certain they worked the same way here. For the first time, I sensed the powerful pathways. If I looked closely enough, I could almost see the glowing lines.

"What are you thinking about? Your energy signature just spiked. It disappeared before anyone could pick up on it, but if it gets worse, we'll need to find a spell to mask you."

"I was thinking about being caught. How can I keep it under wraps?" Everything in the Fae realm was so much more intense.

"Imagine there's a clear cylinder around you. You can see out, but the glass is thick enough to hide you from detection. If you had friends here, you could reach out to them and share energy, so it's felt in various locations throughout the realm."

"We did something like that at my house. My power was split four ways, so I was harder to find."

His head turned my way, and I caught sight of his wide-eyed gaze. "This is a diluted form of your energy? You have to be the most powerful being I've ever met. You can definitely help us beat Vodor and Thelvienne."

I shook my head from side to side. "I'm not all that potent. I think being cut off from them forced the focus back on me entirely. Which way from here?"

We'd reached a crossroads. It was odd because we hadn't been on any discernable path, but here we were at an intersection. Argies glanced around with narrowed eyes as he lifted his head and sniffed the air. It reminded me he could shift into an animal.

"Hey. Why can't you shift forms and fly me there? Are you too small to carry me?"

Argies growled and narrowed his eyes. "I'm bigger than my house in my dragon form, so that makes me easily seen in the sky. Fodor's men are excellent shots. They won't hesitate to take aim if they see a dragon carrying the woman they've been searching for."

"Looks like we're stuck walking then." I should have waited for him to make some tea. Not only did my back hurt, but I was exhausted and dragging ass.

Argies didn't reply. Instead, he wrapped his big hands around my upper arms and took off running. I bounced in his arms as he moved like the wind. The trees passed so quickly I had to squeeze my eyes shut to keep the roller coaster ride happening in my gut from making me puke.

Before I knew it, a fog rolled in like ghosts in the afterworld. Bracing myself for more jarring, I squeezed my eyes shut, tensed, and dug my fingernails into his shoulders. A gasp left me when my back hit the trunk of a tree, and we stopped.

"What's that?" The cold stung my skin where it was exposed. From the second I landed in Eidothea, there had been welcoming energy pulsing from the land beneath my feet. That had shifted to something dark and foreboding.

"Something just crossed into the realm, and if I had to guess, it's frightened Vodor and pissed him off. Many will die before he regains control. We need to get inside before we're sucked into the chaos."

I'd rather be getting a root canal than be here right now. "Ah, so he's throwing a tantrum."

Argies chuckled and set me on my feet, then started walking to the left. "Yeah. A fit that's likely to kill a couple hundred innocent Fae."

I immediately followed him through the trees. We reached a town a few minutes later, and I understood how terrorized this realm really was by their King. Beings of all kinds and ages ran around, trying to get inside.

Argies grabbed my hand and pulled me toward a building that reminded me of my house, only much smaller and one story. There was a sign hanging outside that I couldn't read.

What I did see was the flame rune with its orange glow in the lower right corner.

I looked down the main street and noticed a ripple in the sky a few hundred feet away. "Is that…" My voice trailed off as doors slammed and brownies scurried under homes.

"A death wave? Yes," Argies replied and picked me up before darting inside the home. The sweet yeasty smell of ale told me we were in a tavern. Argies dropped me and went to one of the windows and started drawing runes on the glass. There were others at the remaining windows. When blue light rippled from each of the casters to join in the middle, my ears popped like I was on a plane that just leveled out.

"Let's get some tea and a salad while we wait," Argies suggested.

I nodded and found an empty table where I sank onto a stool. How the hell was I going to get out of here when I couldn't make it more than a few miles before we needed to hole up and hide.

I wanted to know what had the King up in arms. It sounded like a person I needed to be introduced to. I hated that I would leave them in the lurch when they were very clearly suffering, but I had no choice.

You could always stay and leave Ben and Bailey to Violet and Aislinn. I would never forgive myself if I did that. Though I wasn't sure, I would excuse myself when I left these creatures at Vodor's mercy.

This was going to be a long damn day.

CHAPTER 9

"This is not a salad," I argued with Argies as we sat in the pub with about a dozen other Fae. I had no idea how long we'd been here. At some point, while we hid in the bar, I'd started to understand what he meant when he said time moved differently in their realm. But there was nothing I could put my finger on exactly. It was just a feeling I got.

"What would you call it?" He lifted one eyebrow as he held up a fork full of the food.

"I'd call it a garden party. Flowers do not belong among the other veg. And, is there even any dressing on it?" It seemed like maybe there was some oil, but I wasn't sure.

"Those aren't flowers. They're onions, well, our version anyway. And we use citrus and olive oil on our salads. There are also bits of orc in this one."

I picked up one of the tiny daises and brought it to my nose. It smelled like an onion. Nothing here was as it seemed. I popped it into my mouth and chewed. I hadn't realized my face was screwed up until it relaxed, and a smile broke over my mouth.

"Not perfumey at all. Tastes great." I eagerly scooped up a bite and shoveled it into my mouth. The citrus and garlic flavor of the dressing was yummy, and before I knew it, I ate the entire plate.

"Guess we found something here that you like," Argies teased. He reached out and ran his thumb over the corner of my mouth.

The move was too intimate for my taste, and I flinched then stiffened.

Argies held up his hand. "There was a piece of lettuce on your mouth." I saw the yellow fleck on his thumb. It was a relief he wasn't making a pass. The way I'd caught him looking at me several times told me I was wrong, and he was most definitely interested.

This back and forth inside my head was making me slightly ill. Or that could be the fact that my gut churned, and my heart raced. Sitting there and allowing him to touch me like that felt like a betrayal to Sebastian, which was unnerving.

We'd shared some steamy kisses, and I hoped things would go further, but we weren't in a relationship. Were we? We'd never had a conversation about it, so I had no idea how he felt about it.

But I was not built to have multiple love interests. Guilt ate at me, but more than that, I had no desire to play the field. I had always been a one-man girl, but perhaps it was time to shove aside the shame and embrace whoever came my way.

None of that matters right now. Focus on getting home and nothing more. Right. The portal. "How long do we have to hide out in here?"

Argies cleared his throat and set his ale down on the table. "The energy is starting to dissipate. If you tune into your surroundings, I bet you can sense it too."

"I'm not used to looking beyond the obvious unless I'm dealing with a patient in the hospital. I could diagnose a problem inside someone almost as good as a CT scan or MRI." I needed to remind myself I had magic and needed to use it. It hadn't become second nature to me yet.

"It'll get easier the more you tap into your other side. Try it and tell me what you feel."

I nodded my head and closed my eyes to shut out how everyone else in the pub watched us. It unnerved me and made me want to stand up and explain myself. Taking a deep breath, I opened my senses. At first, I felt a light breeze but nothing else. Next came a buzzing noise. It reminded me of what I experienced from the portal, only a million times less intense.

As I focused on that sensation, I realized I'd overlooked the negative energy that permeated everything. It made my skin crawl and sent my heart into overdrive. Now that I'd focused on it, I fought the urge to claw at my flesh like the meth heads in the ER did. There was no doubt in my mind the area was filled with bad mojo, but it couldn't reach into the cracks and crevices inside the buildings.

There was inherent protection in dwellings and businesses given by their owners. Instinctually I had shied away from the negativity and hadn't even realized it. As I paid attention, I felt it retreating little by little until I was able to take a deep breath.

"How the hell do you guys live with that all the time? I couldn't stand it."

Argies sighed and ran a hand through his brown hair. "It's not always this bad. Your arrival set Vodor off and is no doubt pissing Thelvienne off. I'd bet he has her locked inside the castle now, so she can't get to you and suck you dry."

"She could try," I growled. "If she wants to get burned again. Fire is my element, a fact of which I have no problem reminding her." I have no idea why I claimed the element as mine. It wasn't as if I owned fire or anything.

Argies held his hands up. "Don't burn the messenger. But that's something we have in common. I'm fireproof." Flames danced over his fingertips and up to his arms before they disappeared.

"Let's get you some clothes that will help you blend in better. I suspect seeing a foreigner triggered some kind of ward Vodor had set up."

"That would be the smart thing to do, but I don't have any money with me. I didn't expect to get pulled through. Not that you would take money from my realm." I touched my earrings. They were diamond studs Tim bought me for our fifteenth wedding anniversary. The thought of parting with them twisted my stomach in knots.

"These are all I have...aside from this." I pulled the necklace out from under my shirt and held it up. I cringed when I saw the crack. It seemed like this was worthless.

Argies put several coins on the table, making me cringe for not considering how I would pay for the food I ate. "I'm sure the gems will suffice," he told me, making my heartache. "But it won't be necessary. I have the coin to cover the cost."

I shook my head from side to side. "I can't let you do that. I'll use my earrings."

Argies started for the exit, which seemed to be a signal to everyone else. "You can pay me back later. I know those mean something to you. There's no reason to use something with sentimental value."

The sun was bright when we stepped outside. I lifted my hand and shielded my eyes. "I appreciate that. And, I will return and repay the favor. Wow," I blurted when I saw the way Fae flooded out of their homes en masse. "I feel awful for bringing danger to the town."

Argies paused by a store with leather clothes in the

picture window and held the door open for me. "Hey, Phae. I brought someone to have you outfit."

The clomping of hooves sounded before a woman appeared around the doorframe in the back of the shop. She was tall. Easily seven-feet with long auburn hair and hazel eyes. I followed Argies and gasped when the woman entered the front of the store.

Her lower half was that of a horse. I'd never seen a creature like her but recall some like her in movies. "Are you a centaur?"

She chuckled and stopped by a long wooden table. Her front legs stomped the ground several times. "Yes, in fact, I am. Where did you find this one, Argies?"

"Danalise brought her to me. She's the hybrid that came through the portal. Fiona, this is Poniphae. We need some clothes to help her blend in."

I gaped at him, shocked that he told her so much. Potiphar looked out the front window and grabbed hold of my arm. "Let's get you out of these clothes before those soldiers find you."

My heart skipped a beat then took off like a rocket in my chest. I swiveled around and tried to see outside, but she tugged me to the back room. "I'm so sorry for bringing them here. I can sneak out the back. I don't want you to get hurt."

The centaur turned a glower on me and thrust several items of clothing at me. Unlike those in the window, these were made of a soft cotton-like material. "Nonsense. Get these on, and no one will know you don't belong here. Although your energy is pretty distinct. Get changed, and I'll see if Tabitha has a charm to help with that."

Potiphar was trotting to the back door before I could say a word. When she disappeared from view, I shucked my jeans and sweater then stuffed my legs into the dark blue pants.

They reminded me of linen pants, only these were soft as silk. They barely hung on my ample hips. Shrugging, I pulled the top over my head and smoothed the maroon material over my chest. This wasn't quite as big, thanks to my bigger-than-average breasts.

"We're in luck. She had a transformation potion that will shift your energy to mimic another creature."

I looked up from tugging up the bottoms to see a purple liquid in a small vial in the palm of her right hand. "Do you have a belt? I don't want them to fall off."

Phae chuckled and handed me the drink. "I'll adjust them for you."

"Thank you for all your help. I really appreciate it." I held my arms out to my sides, expecting her to bring pins to mark where she needed to sew the new seam. She stared at me for a minute then picked up the sides of the pants. She chanted a foreign word, and the pants shrank around my body immediately until they were as snug as leggings.

"What is the language you spoke just now?"

"It's African. It used to be the only language spoken here, but that changed when our realms meshed. We picked up English, French, and many other languages. Over the years, we started speaking English more and more. Now it's our common language with Alfean being reserved for spell casting," Poniphae explained as she lifted the shoulder of the tunic.

"The top is great. No need to alter it." I had no desire to walk around with my love handles and muffin top on full display. Not that I was ashamed of them. They were symbols of carrying my children.

Argies entered the back room with wide eyes. "They're out front. We need to go, now."

"Drink that," Phae ordered me as she tipped my hand up.

"Act natural. You came to get your mate a new outfit. They won't suspect anything amiss."

I disagreed but had no desire to argue with the centaur. I twisted the top off and smelled the potion. It smelled like strawberries. Thank God. I tipped the liquid back and coughed when I tasted spicy berries.

The liquid slid down my throat despite me hacking up a lung. It burned all the way down, settled in my stomach, and sizzled before bubbles floated throughout my veins, popping along the way.

My head swam, making me dizzy as hell. "Your shoes," Poniphae ordered. I lifted a foot and hopped on my other when I almost fell on my rear end. Strong arms wrapped around my middle. I looked over my shoulder to see Argies holding me.

"This potion has a kick," I informed them both.

Phae removed one shoe, then slid something as soft as my clothes over the foot, set it down, and then lifted my other. "It'll pass as soon as it settles on a form to emulate." Her voice drifted off, and she cocked a brow at Argies behind me.

I didn't pay any attention to that because in the next second, the dizziness passed, and I was fine. "Thank you, Phae. I'll be in touch." Argies handed her a handful of coins then directed me to the front with a hand at the small of my back.

I was still trying to digest everything that had happened when he pulled me outside, and I saw thirty soldiers prowling around the main street. Several approached us holding swords at the ready.

"Can I help you?" Argies asked. "We paid our taxes last week and aren't due until next." I glanced at him and saw he was holding out two cards. I could only see the top one but couldn't read the runes on it.

One of the guards scanned the cards while the other addressed Argies. "Have you seen a hybrid in town?"

"No. We just had a bite to eat and picked up the clothes Phae made for my mate." Argies wrapped his arm around my waist, pulling me close to him. I kept my mouth shut and tried to hide how terrified I was.

Taking slow breaths was not easy, with my heart reaching Indy 500 speeds. My feet wanted to take off running. Good thing I was used to being in stressful situations and not letting my fear show. I plastered a smile on my face and lowered my gaze.

I trained my eyes on the glow surrounding their hands. If I got even a hint that they were going to make a move, I would call upon my magic and do what I could. Potiphar came clomping out of the store at that moment and handed a fabric bag out toward me. "You forgot your tunics. I know how stressful it is when the sweeps happen."

Blood drained from my face as I reached out and took the bag. "It makes me forget my own name." I can't believe we were trying to lie to these soldiers, and neither of us had a bag to show we'd been shopping. Argies had his backpack, but that was it.

"I know how you get. I'll have new fabric in a couple weeks, be sure to come back and see what comes in." Phae turned away without bothering to address anyone else and returned to her store.

"If you see a hybrid female, report her right away," the first soldier ordered before they stalked away.

We walked out of the area in silence and were a quarter-mile away before Argies let go of me and tugged me into the forest that bordered the road. "That was a close call."

"I wasn't worried. The second your energy shifted to match mine, I knew we were going to be fine. Until you took that potion, I was certain you'd be found, and I would be killed."

My jaw unhinged, and I stared at him. "I feel like a dragon right now?"

"Yes, Butterfly. You do." I jumped and turned to the left as a familiar dark voice registered.

"Bas," I called out and leaped into his arms. "What are you doing here?" His familiar hands ran up and down my back as he held me tightly. Immediate fear consumed me as I considered the danger he was putting himself in for me.

"I'm here to take you home."

I pushed on his chest, and he put me down but didn't put more space between us. "How did you know where I was?"

"I waited fifteen minutes then decided to check on you. Isidora told me you'd never made it home. Given that your car was in the driveway, I checked the portal and caught your blood, so I knew you were here. Argies."

The dragon shifter inclined his head. "Sebastian. Good to see you again."

I looked from one to the other. "You two know each other?"

Bas displayed more possessiveness than I'd ever seen from him as he remained within inches of me while his energy exuded from his pores and surrounded me. "We go back a few decades. Are you still heading the rebellion?"

Argies grabbed the fabric bag from me and let his hand linger on my shoulder. "I am. I am taking Fiona back to the portal, but she agreed to return and help our cause."

I felt Sebastian's anger over this before I heard his growl. Ignoring that, I focused on my goal of getting home. "Did you guys find Ben and Bailey?"

Bas shook his head at the same time his forehead furrowed. "Not yet. It hasn't been more than thirty minutes since you left her house."

"Thank God. Hey, if you came through the portal, we can return now." I started walking as if I knew where I was going. Argies grabbed hold of my hand and pulled me to a stop. Sebastian folded his arms over his chest. It would have been nice to have two hot guys vying for my attention, but I was too anxious to really appreciate it fully. I yanked my hand free.

Sebastian's mouth twitched at the edges, telling me he was fighting a grin. Anytime I managed to earn a smile from him was a miracle. He wasn't one to show much mirth, let alone feel it. "No, Fi. We can't get close right now. I cast an invisibility spell before I crossed. I got lucky and landed between some soldiers. Wood nymphs created a distraction across the clearing from me. It's the only reason I managed to get out of the middle of that mess. Without their help, I never would have reached you."

My heart sank to my feet. "What are we going to do?"

"We need to get Vodor to move the soldiers away from that area," Bas announced.

I bobbed my head. "Okay, but how? I don't see a way to make that happen."

Argies ran a hand along the back of his neck. "It'll have to be something big. In a location, the King would never risk you getting a foothold."

Sebastian was nodding his head in agreement. "Precisely what I was thinking. We need to go to Midshield and stage an attack."

A huge smile spread over Argies's face. "Brilliant."

My head swiveled back and forth between them. "Where's Midshield?"

Sebastian smiled at me. "Where the King and Queen live."

"What?!" I screeched.

Bas scooped me up and swung me around. "Don't worry,

Butterfly. We'll never be seen. I know the tunnel system like the back of my hand."

"Wonderful. What are we waiting for? Let's go." I shook my head as I wondered why I trusted him with my life. It was the height of insanity to head into the lion's den like he was suggesting, but I wasn't backing down now.

My best friend was counting on me, and I refused to let her down.

CHAPTER 10

*W*iping the sweat beading on my brow with the back of my hand, I want a hole to open up and swallow me whole. It was beyond embarrassing to be standing there panting like a dog while perspiring like a pig as two of the best-looking men I'd ever laid eyes on stared at me.

Movement in the city before us distracted me from my ridiculous plight. The three of us were standing in an alley close to the edge where the forest met the buildings' brick and stone. And to my surprise, it smelled like every alleyway I'd ever encountered on Earth.

For some reason, I didn't expect to find the cesspool of urine, decay, and mold anywhere in Eidothea. The place had a dark edge to it, but it was clean and free of pollution.

In the distance, three soldiers were dragging a dwarf from his house or his shop. I couldn't tell what the symbol on the window meant. I thought it was something about jewelry but couldn't be sure.

I gasped and rubbed my eyes. "I think my vision is getting

better. Is that possible? Never mind, that was a dumb question. Of course, it isn't. Shit only goes downhill with age."

Sebastian closed the distance between us and tucked a strand of hair behind my ear. "You're thinking in human terms. Remember what I said?"

I lifted one shoulder. There were things I couldn't believe, no matter how much I wanted to. "It doesn't seem possible."

"Set aside your fear of not regaining your youth. You're perfect the way you are. But I do suspect you will see many differences in the months to come. Your magic was suppressed most of your life, so it couldn't inhibit your aging process. Now that you're coming into your power, you will find it halting. I'm just not sure how much can be reversed." Bas took a step back, shattering the moment.

I took a deep breath and turned back to the hustle and bustle. "You're right. I was surprised by seeing the rune on the window behind those soldiers who were harassing the dwarf. We're here in Midshield. Where do we go now?"

Argies stepped up beside Sebastian while scanning the area behind us. "We need to find our way into the tunnels. From there, we will travel to the other side of the city where you can cast a spell to get the soldier's attention."

Bas shook his head. "The best option is to travel around to Steelgate where we enter the hidden areas. It's the only way we can be sure they won't be able to detect her."

I cocked my head. "Not even if Vodor casts that seeking spell or whatever it was?"

Sebastian was in Argies's face in an instant. "You allowed her to be tagged by one of his spells?"

Argies pushed Bas's chest, but he didn't move so much as a muscle. "I protected her and ensured she wasn't detected. I also gave her a safe place to sleep last night."

I got in between them. "This isn't helping anything. We

have shit to do, so if you're done measuring your dicks, I'd like to get to Steel gate and move our plan along."

With a glower, Sebastian grabbed my hand and took off away from the city. I heard Argies following us. The second we stepped into the forest, it felt like a weight lifted from my shoulders.

At first, I assumed it was me releasing the fear of being caught, but I realized it was so much more than that. There was a vampiric shadow over the city. One that sucked the life right out of you. It was that drain that had been weighing on me.

"Have you spoken to your parents since you returned?" Argies's voice startled me. We'd been walking in silence. I was wrapped up in trying to follow the threads of the magic.

Beside me, tension radiated from Bas in hot waves. "No. I haven't."

I tilted my head and looked up at him. "Where are your parents? How long has it been since you've spoken to them?"

He squeezed my fingers then let my hand go. I hadn't meant to offend him and was about to ask more but decided to keep my mouth closed. The fastest way to get someone to open up was to remain silent. Often times they answered your questions just to end an awkward silence.

Sebastian kicked a rock that went sailing through the forest. "My family lives in the Underground of Steelgate, and I haven't spoken to them in nearly seventy years."

"Can I point out that it's been far longer here given the difference in how time moves here?" Argies interjected.

Bas growled low in his throat. The sound was terrifying and made me think of him ripping the dragon to shreds. There was more to this story than I was aware, but I wasn't going to push Bas for more until he was ready.

"Sounds like you're going to get to see and talk to them now. Is there anything you want to warn me about before I get tossed in the deep end?" I stooped to pick a bright purple flower from the ground after asking him to avoid the desire to make eye contact with him.

I was surprised at how silky soft the stem and petals were when I broke it from the plant. When I held it below my nose and inhaled deeply, I noted the sweet scent had some spicy notes as well.

"My father is angry that I left the realm. My brother hates me, and I'm not sure about my mom or sister," Sebastian admitted.

I twirled the flower between my fingertips, trying not to get sucked into fixing Bas's family problems. It was one of my weaknesses. I always jumped into situations where I wasn't necessarily wanted. I wouldn't say a thing when we arrived, but I couldn't leave it entirely alone.

"Family rarely understands the reasons we make the decisions we do, even when it's not their job. And worst yet, they don't bother taking the time to find out. I don't know what happened between you and them, but I know their feelings come from a place of love, regardless of how misplaced it is. The least you can do for them is to acknowledge that. The fact that you can see them and you have a second chance to make things right between you guys is a huge blessing. Believe me, when they're no longer there to talk to you, your history weighs heavily on you." My heart ached for Bas as I tried to get him to see things from a different perspective. I only hoped he didn't think I was too pushy. Tim always thought I lectured him when I was impassioned about something like this.

Sebastian turned his head, and the look in his eyes was filled with emotions that went far beyond his grouchy demeanor. My spine tingled with awareness as his gaze lingered. "Are you hungry?" I wasn't surprised that he didn't respond to my diatribe. He would have to work through it on his own.

Going with his topic shift, I wondered if his question held a hidden meaning. My mind certainly thought so. And to my surprise, my body was on board with stripping the sexy Fae naked then having my way with him. The giant dragon tromping along with us put a damper on the moment and made it easy to yank my mind out of the gutter.

"I'm okay for now. I'm not so sure about the food here. I had a delicious salad this morning, but the food Argies and Danalise gave me last night was awful."

"She didn't care for the dewberries or the fried orc," Argies interjected. "And, she wouldn't try any of the other fruit."

Sebastian chuckled. "I can see why you didn't like the fruit, but orc is kinda like chicken. If it's under or over-cooked, you won't like it. With the right seasonings, you won't be able to tell the difference. We'll eat at the pub Underground. It has the best stew."

Argies made a noise in the back of his mouth. "If you're done making a date, we're here."

Bas glared at the dragon, then turned to a large boulder and shifted it to the side. A dark opening was revealed that made my pulse jump. Vibrant energy, along with too many scents to identify, greeted me as we crossed the threshold. Argies replaced the boulder, taking most of the light as he did.

It took several seconds for my eyes to adjust. When they did, I saw we were in a hall. Noise came from the opposite end, where I could see the tunnel opened up. I followed next to Bas as we headed down the slope to the central part of the cavern.

Within seconds we were standing in an arch leading to a bustling city. I wouldn't have imagined it even existed. The feel down here was so different than on the surface. Nothing was suffocating me. The various energies surrounding me were invigorating.

We were in the middle of a large cave, complete with stalactites coming from the ceiling. It seemed as if they'd removed the stalagmites so they could build their city. There was a mass of two- and three-story buildings in front of us. And there were hundreds of Fae bustling about.

The lighting was provided by massive torches along the stone streets. I could see passages branching off in half a dozen places around the enormous area. Seriously, it was more than three football fields combined.

What struck me first was that the negative energy from the surface didn't touch me here. It was as if there was a shield all around the Underground. The second was the harmony I sensed in the atmosphere. They lived in relative peace with one another.

"The potion is wearing off. We don't have time for dinner unless you want her to be discovered," Argies announced.

"Shit." My hands started shaking, and my stomach twisted into knots. "We need to hurry."

Sebastian shook his head while he started walking to our left. "I'll find my mom. She will have something to shield your identity until we can get to the portal."

"Is that wise? I don't want to risk being stuck here any longer. Violet needs us. Ben and Bailey need us."

Bas grabbed my hand when I stopped walking. I was left with the choice of being dragged by him or moving, so I started walking as well. "You will be discovered the second we step foot in Midshield. We need her help."

Argies was cursing behind us while Sebastian continued into the middle of the city. The buildings weren't very tall, but there were a lot of them. Some had shops on the lower level and homes on the top, while others were homes on both floors. And they all blended together.

He stopped outside one of the residential buildings and stood there looking up at the façade. The door opened, and a woman stepped outside. "Bastian?"

Sebastian's gaze lowered, and his lips thinned. A pained look crossed his face before he tried to smooth it out. "Mother. How are you?"

Two men joined her before she could respond. "What are you doing here?"

"Father. Teagan." Teagan had to be his brother. He looked like their father, where Bas looked more like his mother.

Argies stepped forward. "Kelvhan, Eliyen. Good to see you again. We're here to get Fiona home. She's the hybrid that injured Thelvienne. The King is hunting her, and she needs to return to her realm."

I swallowed as their gazes shifted to me. "I imagine the last thing you want to do is help me, but I have to return and stop whatever is killing Fae in my town. Well, after I rescue my best friend's children. I plan on returning to help overthrow Vodor after Earth is stabilized."

Eliyen, Bas's mom, hurried down the steps and wrapped her arms around her son. "I've missed you." He hugged her back and held her tightly.

When his mom let him go, she remained close to them. "Now, tell me what your plan is."

Sebastian quickly told them what their next steps were while I clasped my necklace and worried it between my fingers. His parents shared a glance before his father joined them. Teagan remained on the porch of their house.

"You aren't heading into Midshield. We will handle that step. You need to go straight to the portal. The opening will be brief, so you will have to act fast," Zelvhan, his father informed them.

I pursed my lips. "How are we going to do that?"

The look his father shot my way bordered on disgust. "We're the leaders of the Underground because we have more power than most."

"Stop it, Zel. She doesn't understand our world. I am going to replicate your power Fiona and deploy it like a bomb in the middle of Midshield while you and my son race to the portal."

I gaped at Eliyen. "You can do that?"

Her head bobbed up and down. "I can."

"But you won't be able to cast a spell to hide Fiona, as well," Sebastian interjected. He rubbed the back of his neck and lowered his head for several seconds. "It's the best solution and will get us there hours faster."

Eliyen extended her hands. "Then let's get started."

I smiled at her and clasped her hands. The second we touched, my skin tingled, and my heart started racing. The electrical current I associated with magic ran over me. Something in my chest unfurled and opened to meet the power surrounding me. Blue light enclosed the two of us for several seconds before releasing me and taking a step back.

"Will you come back with her?" Kelvhan directed his question to Sebastian, who seemed to be in pain.

He gave his father a clipped nod before twining his fingers with mine. "I won't let her return on her own. We need to leave."

His mother hugged him one more time. He didn't let go of me, so I was close enough to hear her shuddering breaths. I wasn't surprised to see her face shining with tears when they parted.

"Tell Chasianna I said hi, and I will see her when we return." Sebastian inclined his head in his father and brother's direction, but they remained silent.

Argies was in motion before we were. I had assumed he

was returning home, but Bas moved to follow him, proving I was wrong. We hurried through the Underground and traveled through a different passage than the one we entered.

Sebastian paused at the stone blocking our exit. I took a moment to see if I could sense the negative energy and was surprised when I couldn't pick up the slightest tendril. Whatever seal they had down there, it was airtight.

"We have to move fast as soon as I open the door," Bas told her.

"How do we know when to go?" Right as I asked that dirt sprinkled from the ceiling onto our heads. Was that from a mass exodus of soldiers above us?

I never got a chance to ask that as Argies shoved the stone aside, and Bas was running through the doorway into the forest. He still had hold of my hand and was pulling me with him. I yanked my hand free and managed to extricate myself without falling.

Argies was beside me a second later. The pounding of hooves could be heard nearby as we ran. I couldn't tell where anything was. We could be headed right for the guards for all I knew. I trusted Argies and Sebastian to get us to safety, or I would have stopped moving long enough to get my bearings.

Movement near the trees caught my eye, and I noticed wood nymphs joining us along with brownies and other creatures as we ran. It was unreal to be running in the Fae realm alongside so many different beings.

I could see the clearing up ahead but couldn't tell if soldiers were still there. Sebastian barreled right through the tree line and into the open. I continued running until I saw him fighting with several guards. I stopped so suddenly that Argies ran into my back and knocked me down.

He tripped over my prone body and joined me on the ground. I pushed my upper body up, but before I could get to my feet, a foot connected with the side of my head. I went flying to the left as pain exploded inside my skull.

I tried to fire off a spell to combat the soldiers coming at me, but nothing happened. The power I'd felt buzzing through my veins seemed to go dormant. *Now?! You choose now to go on the fritz?* As my mind raced and my breaths turned choppy, I scolded myself.

Keep it together, Shakleton. Mind over magic. Slowing my breaths, I reminded myself I was the most powerful witch in Cottlehill Wilds. Nothing, and no one was going to take that from me. The tingling started up in my fingers and spread from there. A smile spread across my face.

Climbing to my feet, I resolved to make the portal my bitch. I was the Guardian. To my surprise, tendrils of magic from the portal brushed across my skin as soon as my resolve settled. It was here and waiting on me. I had to get it open and crawl through before these soldiers killed us.

"Pretentious." The word didn't come out as forcefully as I wanted, but it did the job.

In the middle of the clearing, a multicolored oval shimmered about two feet off the ground. I heard a snarl and turned in time to see Argies toss a soldier at a group of dwarves I hadn't noticed until that moment.

"Fiona!" Sebastian's voice was tinged with fear and warning. Following instinct, I curled into a ball and rolled away. Clumps of dirt exploded a foot from me.

Thankfully it had missed, and I was on my feet a second later. I conjured fireballs and tossed them at the guard that was attacking me. It hit him in the chest, and he quickly became engulfed in flames.

I ran full out for the image of the crypt in my family cemetery. Energy buzzed around me the closer I got. A soldier came at me from the side, and I tossed another fireball. This one missed, but it did force the guy to duck which gave me the opening I needed.

Without thought, I ran and jumped, aiming myself for the middle of the portal. My body hit something, and the same darkness encompassed me that happened when I went through the first time.

My hair whipping around my head, and the wind stole my ability to breathe. I would never get used to traveling via the portal. I felt more than I saw the dark tunnel as I was pulled through it.

This time, the one thing that was different was that my trip passed quickly, this time, unlike last time when it felt as if I was in there for an eternity. A bright light flashed, blinding me as the compression surrounding me vanished, and I was unceremoniously dropped onto the hard ground of the crypt.

Scrambling to my feet, I turned and shouted Sebastian's name. I watched as Argies was thrown toward the portal by a soldier. His name left my lips next as I prayed he wasn't injured.

The second his body made contact with the portal, my internal sensor pinged. Immediately I knew it was him and was glad when my gut told me he meant me no harm. Eidothea hadn't broken me.

"You can cross. Grab Bas if you can."

The dragon stumbled through and fell at my feet, but I couldn't look away from the fight Sebastian was embroiled in. The guard pulled a sword and had sliced him at some point. Blood poured from his side and one arm.

Bas bared his teeth and blocked the sword, earning another cut. I wanted to scream and was about to jump back through to help him when he grabbed hold of the weapon and swung it in a circle.

The muscles along the sides of his neck bulged as he

moved. Blood sprayed as the blade sliced through the flesh of two soldiers. Their heads went one direction while their bodies collapsed to the ground.

Sebastian didn't waste any time as he dropped the sword and leaped through the portal. My sensor pinged, and I gave him permission to cross, as well. I caught him when he fell through.

He was covered in blood and had more cuts than a birthday cake, but we were both alive, and we were home.

"Let's get your injuries cleaned so we can head back to Violet's house."

Bas grunted and glared at the dragon bracing himself on the wall of the mausoleum. These two were going to come to blows at some point. I didn't have time for their pissing match. I hadn't slept in days, and I hadn't eaten either. And I didn't have time to do either at the moment. I needed to talk to Grams and patch Bas up, then locate Ben and Bailey.

Just another day in my magical life.

CHAPTER 11

"*L*ooks like it's my turn to play host to you," I told Argies as I headed for the exit. Sebastian was at my side, but the dragon shifter remained in place as he stared at the spot the portal had just closed.

"It's not safe for you to return right now. It'll do no one any good if you get killed." Sebastian's words were growled at Argies and riled him up, but I suspected it was on purpose. Argies turned away and glowered at Bas as he stalked past him.

"Fuck off, Stankeld. I've managed to keep things progressing despite your absence. I don't need you butting in now."

Bas sighed and reached out for me but let his hand drop. Things were suddenly awkward between us, and I wasn't as sure of his feelings toward me. I didn't have much experience with dating and relationships, and I never expected to be in this position in my mid-forties.

What was worse was that I hadn't been this uncertain about myself since my face resembled a pizza and my breasts were just developing.

"Let's go talk to Isidora so we can get back to Violet." Sebastian stalked out without waiting for me.

With a sigh, I left the crypt and almost laughed when I saw both men standing at the entrance to the cemetery facing opposite directions. "Who's up for coffee and tarts?"

Argies turned my way. His wrinkled forehead, pinched lips, and creased eyes told me it was his turn to be confused by what I offered. "Tarts are a type of pastry. Usually filled with custard and topped with fruit. Not the moldy flower-flavored ones you have in Eidothea, but ones that actually taste good," I explained to him as I trudged up the stairs.

I opened the back door and kicked off the soft moccasin-like shoes in the mudroom. They'd been extremely comfortable, especially given all the running and fighting we'd done.

"Grams!" I called out as I entered the kitchen.

She came zipping through the wall that separated the kitchen and the living room. "Where have you been? I have been going out of my mind, and I couldn't do anything to find out what happened."

I fought the urge to lower my head and apologize. She always had a way of making me feel bad if I ever made her worry. "Did you feel it when I was sucked through the portal?"

"Is that what happened?" I'd never known her not to know something. She usually knew things before I even did.

I bobbed my head up and down as I turned on the coffee maker. "Long story short, yes." I reached up and touched the necklace under my top. I didn't feel the crack anymore and pulled it out to check.

The crack was indeed gone. The gem on top was once again seamless, but it was no longer amber like it was initially. The section down the middle where the jewel had broken reminded me of the aurora borealis with green, blue, purple running blending together. And the entire thing glowed.

I glanced up at Sebastian, who looked at me with wide eyes. Grams hovered over my shoulder, checking it out, as well. "What did you do to my granddaughter to make this charm hold both of your magic? And, who is this dragon?"

"This is Argies. He's the leader of the rebellion in Eidothea," I explained, ignoring the topic of my necklace and the fact that it now contained a combination of my magic and Sebastian's.

Sebastian grunted as he retrieved my favorite mug and a couple pods to put into the machine. "My father leads the uprising. Argies works with him."

"None of that matters right now. I want to hear how you were pulled through the portal." Thankfully, Grams had been distracted from the topic of my charm and was more worried about other events.

I swallowed the lump in my throat and told her what had happened when I entered the crypt earlier. Grams started pacing. Well, more like she floated back and forth rapidly in the same pattern.

"He was coming through with Vodor's help. The fact that he couldn't break through is a good sign. You're mastering control over the portal. But bad that the King is strong enough to have his minions even get a pinkie through." Grams was right. I was mastering my ability to control the portal. The image of it appearing upon my call popped into my mind.

"We will deal with reinforcing protections, but first, I need to ask you about working around blocks when scrying."

Before Grams could answer, the door opened, and Violet and Aislinn rushed through.

"Fiona. Thank the Gods, you're okay. We were worried

something happened to you when you didn't return," Violet blurted as she pulled me into her arms.

"How long have I been gone?" I glanced at the clock and noticed only an hour or so had passed.

Aislinn glanced around wide-eyed. "Not long. We came because both of us sensed you were in danger."

Grams floated closer with a smile on her face as she interrupted what Aislinn was saying. "That's because you three have formed a coven and your bond is strong. In fact, I'd say you're far more powerful than Camille's coven of thirteen is."

I shared a look with Aislinn and Violet. I shrugged my shoulders. Apparently, the rivalry between my Grams and Camille would never end. Aislinn nodded in silent agreement before she continued. "What happened?"

I sighed and released Violet to fix my cup of coffee while I introduced Argies, then told them the events from the time I was pulled through to the Fae realm. "There's suspicion a bilge is killing Fae here and could be responsible for kidnapping the kids."

Grams gasped and turned red around the edges at the same time her glow became brighter. "We need to find it right away."

Sebastian got up into Argies's face. "Are you certain it's a bilge?" I swear Bas's muscles seemed to swell, and he got even bulkier.

Argies was unaffected by the display. "I can't say for sure. It's the first thing that came to mind when Fiona told me the scene of the last killing was staged to look like a dragon did it."

"I hadn't wanted to consider something so vile beings in our realm," Sebastian admitted.

I held up my hand. "I still don't understand why everyone

gets worked up over a bilge. Can someone please explain that to me?"

Something cold tickled my ear, and I turned to find my Grams hunched over, staring at me. "What?" That came out harsher than I expected.

Grams cocked her head as her gaze traveled over my face. "You've been changed by your trip to Eidothea."

My mouth opened, then closed. I traced my cheeks then moved over my head. I stiffened and shot my friends a wide-eyed look when I touched the tips of my ears. "Are they pointed now?"

Violet nudged my hair out of the way and pursed her lips. "Not like a full-blooded Fae."

My head snapped to Sebastian, wondering why his ears weren't pointed. "I use a glamour to ensure they aren't seen." Bas muttered something I couldn't hear, then the air shimmered around him, and I got my first glimpse of his pointed ears.

"Why have mine changed?"

"The magic of the Fae realm brought out that side of your heritage. You've even lost a few of the age spots." Aislinn's hand flew to her mouth like she'd said something wrong. I was okay with losing some liver spots. I could lose the hot flashes and knee pain, too.

I inhaled and shook my head. "There's always something to make my head spin. That doesn't matter right now. We need to come up with a plan to identify what we're facing and find a way to locate Ben and Bailey."

"Oh, thank the Gods. I thought I was going to have to go it alone while you dealt with all of this." Tears brimmed in Violet's eyes as she blurted her relief.

I wrapped my arms around her and held her close. "You'll never be alone in anything. I've got your back."

"So do I. Ride or die, bitches!" Aislinn announced with a

fist pump into the air, then her expression sobered as she laid her hand on Violet's back. "We will find them."

I let go of Violet and crossed to the fridge, and pulled out the tart. "This is what fruit should taste like. Not that moldy dirt you tried to pass off."

Sebastian reached around me and snatched a raspberry from the top of the desert. I smacked his hand then placed the slice on a plate Aislinn set in front of me. She added a fork and gave it to Argies.

Argies made a humming noise that made me smile as I dished a piece of the tart to Bas, then Violet and Aislinn. "Okay this is delicious," the dragon admitted. "But to be fair, you didn't get to experience much from my realm."

"I tasted enough," I informed him, then took a bite. The flaky crust combined with the creamy filling and sweet fruit exploded on my tongue. I felt renewed as the caffeine took effect and the food-filled my belly.

"Grams, do you have any ideas on how we can locate the kids or the Fae responsible for killing here?" So much had happened since I called her spirit back to this realm, and I hadn't been able to take advantage of having her here.

"I'm not certain there will be a spell powerful enough to overcome whatever is blocking your scrying. I think a different approach will be more successful. You need to tackle it from an angle the caster couldn't have anticipated. As for who is killing in our town, that's another beast altogether. I have a feeling whoever is responsible will find you eventually."

My blood froze, and the tart curdled in my stomach. I could deal with blood, guts, and gore, but this hidden danger was another story altogether. Think of it like battling cancer. You just need the right arsenal. *Chemo.* I needed the magical version of chemotherapy and radiation treatment. Nothing can withstand that level of toxicity.

CHAPTER 12

"I don't need to go anywhere. I don't know anyone here, and I have no desire to leave Fiona alone." The smirk on Argies's face told me he knew exactly how much he was annoying Sebastian. The two of them didn't get along at all, and it didn't help that Argies had not hidden his interest in me. Although, it seemed as if he was far more interested in Aislinn, or maybe even Violet. He kept eyeing them both like a hungry predator.

I had no idea what his life was like in Eidothea. Perhaps he didn't spend much time considering relationships or pursuing women. From what I saw of life in the Fae realm, there wasn't much fun. It was a lot of running, fear for your power, and a deep-seated hatred for the kingdom's leaders.

Bas glared at the dragon shifter. "So, you're saying you won't help me talk to the residents about what they've seen? I'm still convinced someone had to have seen something when Ben and Bailey were taken. Even a bilge would be hard-pressed to maintain complete control over those two at the same time."

I smiled at the thought. Violet's children were a force to

be reckoned with. "No one would talk to us when we tried earlier, but you garner so much more respect than a bunch of middle-aged women."

Sebastian turned his narrowed eyes on me. "You're thinking like a human again."

My cheeks heated, and my throat clogged up, making it impossible to respond. Violet came to my rescue. "Her point is valid in that we are seen as women and of little power. There's a gender bias even in the supernatural world."

Grams turned red around the edges. "She's not wrong. I fought against it my entire life. You'll show them precisely why they're wrong, Fiona."

I nodded my head. "You should talk to Mae. She's hears everything in this town. If I didn't know better, I'd say it was one of her abilities."

Grams waved her hand and shook her head. Thankfully, her edges had lost the red tinge. "She sticks her nose in everyone's business. She doesn't care if it's rude to ask Fiona if she kissed Sebastian. And people tell her because she throws them off by inquiring in the first place."

My face heated for the second time in as many minutes. "We get it, Grams. She doesn't conform to social norms. It seems if anyone saw anything, she'd be likely to have heard about it."

Sebastian closed the distance between us and lifted my hand to his lips, then kissed the back of it. "We will talk to her first. Do you need Camille for the spell?"

I was shaking my head when Grams floated right up to us. "Hell no, we don't need that woman. Fiona and the girls have me. She was helpful before Fiona called me back, but I'm here now."

I turned to face Grams, wishing I could wrap my arms around her. "And, I am beyond grateful Fate allowed you to return. I'm sorry I wasn't here more before. I should have come more often. Maybe if I was here, I could have stopped whatever…" I trailed off, unsure what exactly happened to Grams. There was no outright information that indicated she had been killed, but my gut told me that is precisely what happened.

Grams reached out and stroked my cheek. A cold sensation registered right before her hand went through me. "If you had been here, you would likely have been killed right along with me. I should have told you much sooner who you really were. Then you'd have been better prepared."

"Why didn't you tell me after my parents died? I get that you were obeying their wishes, but why not once they were gone?"

She snorted, which coming from a ghost, was an eerie sound. "You'd have thought I lost my mind. You are a scientist at heart and would have assumed I was suffering from Alzheimer's or dementia and tried to have me moved into a psychiatric hospital. You weren't here enough for me to show you, so I would have had to tell you over Skype. No way was I going to do that."

"We've talked about how she needed to live her own life and come here of her own accord. If she'd felt like she had no choice but to become the next Guardian, she would have resented the burden." I gaped at Sebastian, unsure what surprised me more. The fact that they'd talked about me or that they assumed I would have been upset about needing to take Gram's place.

I opened my mouth to give them a scathing rebuke only to clamp it shut. They were absolutely right. I would have felt obligated, and it would not have settled well with me. "I'll give you that one. None of that matters now, anyway. What's done is done. We have more important matters to deal with now. Hopefully, when you get back, we will have some answers."

Bas scooped me into his arms and kissed the breath out of me before setting me back down and giving me a knowing look. He was staking his claim on me and making it known. A sensual heart unfurled through me as I watched them walk out the door.

"Well that was the hottest thing I've seen in a long time," Aislinn blurted.

When I was younger, that statement would have had me wanting to crawl into a hole. Now, I didn't have the energy or desire to be embarrassed. "He's talented," I replied with a shrug. "And, he has a sweet side few ever see. Although his grumpiness is what drew me to him in the first place."

Violet made a choking sound. "I think you're the first person in history to use sweet and Bas in the same sentence. There's no doubt you two are made for each other."

"I prefer my men smiling," Aislinn interjected.

I smirked at her. "Argies smiles a lot. And, he's pretty sexy, too."

"I'm not in the market. I learned my lesson long ago that I'm better off alone. No men for me, thank you." Aislinn's attitude toward relationships was far more familiar to me than I cared to admit.

Most women my age feel that way, especially after a nasty divorce. I felt that way, and still do, in no small degree, but for very different reasons. I had a loving marriage and lost him and have been in no hurry to find someone new. I wanted to focus on myself for once.

A high percentage of middle-aged women eschew new partners because their previous ones have been awful to them. Why invite another man to mistreat them? Besides the fact that when we go through a terrible loss, whether it's from divorce or death, it brings into sharp focus what you have neglected to do for yourself in deference to another.

"Understandable. We need to focus on Ben and Bailey

before the rest of the town right now, anyway. Let's try to combine power and sneak past whoever is hiding the kids from us." The more I talked, the more confident I felt. This would work. We were incredibly powerful and more intelligent than most.

Violet and Aislinn followed me to the attic, where I opened the window and allowed in the breeze, but also the moonlight. I inhaled deeply, grateful to be back inside my home.

"Be sure to light the white candles. And, add a dark purple one for intuition. Oh, and a black one for a couple reasons," Grams threw out there, cutting me off with a look. I have no idea how she knew I was about to object to the use of black candles. "Black is most often associated with protection which Ben and Bailey need, but it's also about uncrossing the magic blocking you. Not to mention it can be used to ward off any negativity that may be sent your way."

"I have so much to learn." I sighed and grabbed the candles Grams mentioned while Violet drew a circle with salt. After I placed the candles, the three of us formed a circle and clasped hands.

Violet cast the circle, which activated with a bright flash of white light. The atmosphere buzzed with renewed vitality. My skin tingled, and I swore I could take the King and Queen on by myself at that moment. Okay, not entirely alone, seeing as my two best friends were the reason, I was so pumped.

Something Grams said clicked, and instead of scrying like usual, I did something else. "*Acies.*" The air condensed, and I focused on my desire to get a glimpse of the kids and their location.

When nothing happened several minutes later, I dropped their hands and rubbed the back of my neck. "Well that didn't work. Any other ideas of how we can think outside the box?"

Aislinn released the lip she'd been chewing on and sighed. "What about doing a mind-meld with Bailey. Not sure I want to see what a seventeen-year-old boy thinks."

Violet's mouth tipped up at the corners. "Ben's head is a terrifying place. Seriously, Bailey and I are always saying he isn't right in the head. Although at the moment, I'm fairly certain Ben is thinking about how he can save his sister from their predicament."

"You'll need some lavender to align your third eye and some blur lotus to open your crown chakra." Grams was near the bookshelves containing her jars of herbs. Violet released the circle to grab both items and a metal bowl, then returned and cast their magic again.

Placing the dried plants in the container, she lit them then motioned Aislinn and me over. We clasped hands, and the smoke rose to our faces. It was sweet and bitter at the same time. Initially, I became sleepy but quickly got over that.

Violet took a deep breath and chanted, "*Commisceo*." I kept Bailey forefront in my mind the entire time, hoping to get anything from her.

Several seconds later, I struggled to breathe through the terror and agony traveling through my left ankle. I gasped and clutched my leg. In the process, I let go of Aislinn and Violet.

Reality rushed back to me, and the sensations vanished. "Grab my hands. There was something there. I think her…"

"Ankle is hurt," Aislinn said, cutting me off. She snatched my hand then Violet's.

I choked up when I noticed the tears brimming in Violet's eyes. She was far more put together than I would be in her place. Pretty sure I would be a blubbering mess the second my kids went missing.

Violet cast the spell once we were connected again. Only this time, nothing happened. We waited for long agonizing minutes, but nothing came through.

"Let me try another one," I suggested. They both nodded, and I gathered myself and searched for another way around merging. "*Misce*."

For nearly a full minute after I cast the spell, nothing happened. The air had lost all its vibrance and was now oddly empty. And my skin no longer tingled. Crap. "That's not working. Anyone else have anything?"

"I think I have one. I just need a minute to recenter my mind. I don't want my fear of failing Violet and the kids to cause any problems." Aislinn's words were a potent reminder of where we should be focused. And that time I hadn't kept Bailey at the front of my mind. I hadn't been thinking about much of anything, really.

While Aislinn composed herself, I did the same. My children meant everything to me, and I know Ben and Bailey were Violet's entire world, as well. I pictured Bailey's brilliant smile and bright blue eyes. She looked so much like her mom.

And her voice. I swear she and Violet had siren in their blood somewhere. Ever since I'd known Violet, she had been able to make you do anything she asked of you. And, boys always flocked to her. Bailey was the same way.

"Are you part siren?" The words were out before I could stop them. Violet's eyes widened a bit then her cheeks turned pink. "I don't announce it. I can't influence anyone like my grandmother could."

"Could have fooled me," Aislinn teased. "Why do you think your store is so successful in this day and age of electronic books?"

Violet shrugged her shoulders. "I'm okay with that. I have no problem selling them something that will enrich their lives. Hey, maybe I should try to talk to Bailey and tell her to talk her way out of captivity!"

I shook my head. "She might be successful in that, but I'd rather we save her. It's the only way I can be sure her influence over her captor doesn't slip. Because if she tried and somehow lost control before she was safe, she would pay the price. That's too much to put on her."

"All right," Aislinn murmured as she grabbed my hand again. I cleared my mind and thought only about Bailey and her sass.

"*Inquinatae!*" Aislinn's voice seemed to reverberate around our circle. Everywhere it touched, it buzzed and bubbled with vigor. My skin was tingling again. I braced myself for the pain, so it wasn't a punch to the gut when it registered.

I tried to glean anything I could from her surroundings. I heard water dripping somewhere. At first, I thought it was a cave, but the ping told me that wasn't right. It was a sink. I couldn't smell anything, and before I could gather any more information, all sense of her was gone.

Before I could register, the desire to reconnect images started shuffling through my head. First, I saw a black dog jumping through Violet's picture window before it latched onto Bailey's leg. The creature had leather-like skin and red eyes.

Several came through next. Ben being hit with a tail, followed by him being dragged through what looked like a portal. The next thing I saw were imps with long pointy ears and massive noses. I thought I saw the flash of a sofa. It passed too fast to determine if it was like Argies's or something I would find on Earth.

Chains floated toward me as the black dog transformed into a dark-skinned bald man. He waved a finger through the air, and the metal links followed his command and wrapped around Ben first, who had been bucking and kicking imps into the walls. Bailey had gone stock still when her brother started being chained up.

Tears fell down her cheeks a second later, but she remained in place while she was chained to a wall. All I could see was grey stone surrounding them. The lights overhead were incandescent. Between one blink and the next, they were gone.

I looked from Aislinn to Violet and squeezed her hand. "They're still on Earth. We're one step closer to them. We just need to try again. Grams was right. Tackling this from another angle is going to get us there."

"Of course, I was right, child. I'm always right." Gram huffed and lifted her chin in the air.

I lifted one eyebrow as I stared her down. "You weren't right about keeping me in the dark."

She sent me a dark look that made me want to lower my head and apologize. No matter how old I got, the urge to please her never went away. "You should try *iugo*. That will join you together."

Violet bobbed her head. "I bet with that I will be able to maintain a connection."

I took a deep breath and decided to focus on the connection between mother and daughter. Violet was our best bet at locating them. Violet chanted the spell, and the air crackled around us.

The sensation intensified, and I expected to start seeing something any second. My gaze shifted from Aislinn to Violet as I waited. It became clear nothing was coming to Aislinn or me. Just when I was about to let go, I noticed how Violet's eyes had gone distant.

It seemed like forever as we stood there holding hands while Violet spaced out. It reminded me of someone having an absence seizure. When it continued for several minutes, I reassured myself she wasn't a child and had never shown any signs of a seizure disorder.

Finally, she blinked and shook her head. I couldn't wait for a second longer. "Are you alright? Did you see them? Do you need tea or anything?"

Violet let go of our hands and went to take a step but ended up stumbling like she was a newborn foal. "I." She paused and cleared her throat. "I saw them. Let's get tea, and I will tell you all about it."

"I'll get it started. You guys take your time coming down," Aislinn offered.

I was so lucky to have these women in my life. I couldn't ask for more. "Thank you."

I stayed close to Violet and took the stairs slowly. By the time we made it to the kitchen, three mugs of steaming tea and some cookies were on a plate. Grams followed us down and remained quiet while Violet sipped her drink.

"Are they okay?" Grams' voice cracked on the question. The first sign I'd seen at how this impacted her.

Violet nodded her head and set her cup down. "I saw them in a large house. It was old. The furnishings were antiques and in desperate need of repair. The windows were filthy, and I couldn't see anything from Bailey's position. Still, I heard cars driving and honking, sirens, and shouting. I'd bet my left tit they're in a city."

My heart leaped in my chest. "That's good. Do you think they are in London?"

Violet looked up at me, and I could see she wasn't smiling like I was with the news. "I have no idea. I didn't see anything to indicate where in the world they were."

"Were they speaking English? Outside I mean. If they weren't, we might be able to narrow down the search that way." I prayed she said no. It sounded like Japanese or something. That would significantly narrow our search.

"Yes, they were speaking English. And, I think they might not have had an accent like yours. It was tough to tell. I didn't catch words, per se. I got the feeling more than anything. But, maybe that's enough."

I wrapped an arm around her shoulders. "Your impressions are always spot on. We'll start in London since it's the biggest city in England and go from there."

"Perhaps you'll be able to sense them when we close in," Aislinn added.

Violet latched onto that and sat forward, reaching for Aislinn's hand. "Yes. I'm sure I'll be able to. I've never felt closer to Bailey in my life. I know I will sense her."

I would do anything to ensure Violet got the chance to prove her point. "I'll call Camille to keep an eye out and let Bas know we're heading to the city." I pulled out my phone to make the calls, praying we weren't starting a wild goose chase.

CHAPTER 13

"I'm not sure this was the best idea," Aislinn said for the hundredth time since we left Pymm's Pondside.

I sighed and turned in my seat until I was facing Aislinn and could see Violet from the corner of my eye. I still wasn't used to having the driver's seat on the opposite side of the car, so Aislinn agreed to drive into the city. The last thing we needed was for me to get flustered and end up in a crash.

"What would you have us do? Ben and Bailey are in a city. London is the closest one for us to check while Violet continues trying to get more information from Bailey."

Aislinn glanced over at me. "We should have waited for Bas and Argies. They could help us."

My gut churned. They were going to head toward us the second they saw the note we left them. "You're right, but we don't have time to waste. If they aren't in London, we will need to regroup."

"They're there," Violet informed us. "I know it with every cell in my body."

I shifted, so I was looking directly at her. "Have you seen anything else?"

She bobbed her head. "It wasn't much, but I caught sight of what looked like average townhouses. They had red brick and white trim."

Aislinn cursed under her breath. "That could be anywhere in just about any city."

"But even I know the importance of listening to your gut. Especially when it comes to your children. I've seen mothers and fathers push for more testing when they refused to believe doctors couldn't find anything wrong with their son or daughter, and it ended up saving the kid's life."

Aislinn lifted her hands from the wheel for a second. "You're right. I don't have kids, so I wouldn't know anything about that."

"I understand being frightened about facing the unknown, but it will take us some time to locate the building. I have no doubt Sebastian and Argies will be heading our way before we know it." I considered calling Bas and having him drop what he was doing to leave now. They really wouldn't be that far behind us then.

"You're right. So, where should we start? The North West side of London where we will come in from?" Aislinn drummed her fingers on the steering wheel as she drove down the quiet highway. It was dark, so I didn't see much of the beautiful countryside.

"Head to the center of the city. From there, I should get a sense of which direction to head." Violet sounded distant as she spoke, and I wondered if she was bracing herself for the worst or if she was distracted by trying to connect with Bailey. If I knew it was the former, I would try to get her thinking positively, but I didn't want to interrupt if it was the latter.

I decided to keep my mouth shut, and we drove in silence

for several long seconds. When lights came into view in the distance, my muscles started jumping, and my heart skipped s few beats.

I rubbed my hands on my jeans when tingling started up in my hands. "Are there any pockets of supernaturals in the city? I was thinking perhaps like would attract like, and they'd live near one another. That might narrow down where we should start looking."

Aislinn glanced over at me. "Not really, no. The city has too many humans for our kind to feel comfortable. All those bodies tend to block the flow of energy from the ley lines to a larger degree than living away from densely populated areas."

"The clusters we will find in and around the city will all be along those magical pathways," Violet interjected. "But, Aislinn's right. There isn't a huge population here. Besides the fact that most of our kind thrive on nature and our connection to it. You don't get as much of a boost when your exposure to the source is limited."

I sat forward as we hit the outskirts of London. "That makes sense. Is there a magical market here where we can ask questions? We might be able to find out if anyone's seen anything suspicious. Or felt anything nefarious."

Aislinn slowed the car and bobbed her head while remaining focused on the road ahead. Traffic had increased as we got closer, and now there were vehicles all around us. "That's a good idea. We can start at The Tenth Ring. It's the market in St. James park across from Buckingham Palace."

"Sounds good to me," I agreed. Violet didn't say anything, but I noticed her wring her hands together and chew on her lip. Aislinn exited the highway and made so many turns that I got lost. That wasn't all that surprising since I hadn't been there nearly enough to know where anything was.

My phone vibrated in my pocket, and I pulled it out.

Seeing Sebastian's name flash on the screen made my pulse quicken for polar opposite reasons. Both were understandable, but it was odd to have excitement and fear racing through me in equal measures.

"Hello."

"Fiona," Sebastian growled from the other end of the connection.

"Did you even read my note? We still have no idea precisely where they are being held. Violet is convinced they're here in London. We are starting our search at The Tenth Ring. If we're lucky, we will have a location by the time you and Argies get here."

"Don't go into any building until we reach you guys. You haven't honed your craft enough to anticipate the best counterattacks."

I hated that he was right. Not that I planned on telling him that. "I am not a liability anymore. I can burn anything to a crisp. We will see you soon." I hung up before he could say anything else. I expected him to call back, but he didn't.

By the time I shoved my cell in my back pocket Aislinn was pulling up to the curb. We were close to a memorial for a previous queen of England. I had never been to this part of town. It was beautiful at night. When we all climbed out, I saw the park down the street.

I was about to ask if leaving the car was a good idea when she cast a spell to hide the vehicle. I loved magic. It made life so much more enjoyable. While it made most things easier, it also created problems.

There were more people out and about than I expected at this time of night. I would have thought most would be eating dinner either at home or in restaurants. When we entered the park and got close to the blue bridge, I noticed Fae popping out of the shadows.

"What the hell?" I grabbed Violet's hand and slowed her down.

Violet patted my hand and let go of me. "Don't worry, most of them are hidden from humans."

I cocked my head and watched a brownie run right in front of a couple walking down one of the main trails. "Is that what the greenish outer glow is about?"

"Yep," Aislinn replied as she hurried closer to us.

"What are those?" I'd never seen the small, slimy creatures crawling out of the lake in the middle of the park. It looked a little like a mole crossed with a lizard and was dark green, almost black.

One side of Violet's mouth lifted in a sneer. "Those are squonks. Nasty, smelly creatures. The market is on the other side of the bridge."

The energy of the park was soothing, but nothing as vibrant as I experienced in Cottlehill Wilds. The water was still with the moonlight shining off the surface, but I didn't see anything under the surface.

Once we reached the other side, a gnarled older woman glared at us from between two trees. All I could see was her silver hair and her navy skirt and oversized, flowing maroon top. Violet headed right for her. "We're searching for a *bilge*. Have you seen one in the city?"

We stopped a few feet from her, and I realized she wasn't sitting on a bench like I thought. She was merely short. This close, I could see her stormy gray eyes. Her most telling feature, aside from her antagonistic energy, was that she looked more like a raisin than anything else.

"You don't belong here. Go home." Her voice was like a leaf rattling in the wind. It wasn't terrifying, but it didn't sound human either, which I found odd. Her energy was closer to Violet, making me assume she was a witch.

Aislinn bared her teeth at the lady. "We aren't going home

until we do what we came for, witch. You'd be wise not to mess with our coven. The Backside of Forty isn't known for their tolerance."

The old lady threw her head back and cackled. Her laughter died down, and she said a word that had the hairs on my arms standing on end. I reacted without thinking. "*Obclusus!*"

The witch's voice cut off, and Violet turned wide eyes to me. "What did you do?"

I shrugged my shoulders. "Shut her up. She was calling out for backup."

Aislinn got right in the woman's face. "That's how the Backside of Forty handles shit. If anyone ever breaks that spell and you get your voice back, be sure to tell everyone you know."

Violet tugged me in the opposite direction at a fast clip. Aislinn was right behind us. I saw a ripple in the distance and assumed it was the market, but when imps appeared out of nowhere with weapons drawn, we took off running. We made our way through the park and out onto the street.

We were heading away from our car, so we couldn't jump in it and take off. My knee was throbbing, and my lungs burned, but I wasn't ready to collapse just yet. It was one thing to be in shape physically and another to be able to escape violent beasts chasing you.

I yanked on Violet's arm when we turned a corner, leaving the park behind. "What do we do now?"

"We keep moving. V, you need to keep your 'momdar' on as we move through the streets. Maybe we'll get lucky and find them." Aislinn wasn't even winded as we raced along the pavement. I remember what it was like to be under forty. Oh, to be young again.

"It's hard to sense them when I'm running for my life...oof." Violet jolted to a stop and windmilled her arms when she ran into a guy as we turned yet another corner. She was slightly ahead of us, close to what I thought was St. Paul's Cathedral. I'd been there once when I was a kid.

I braced her back from behind and barely stopped myself from running into her back. Aislinn paused right beside me. I wasn't sure what alerted me to danger, but I grabbed hold of Violet and pulled her around the guy.

The guy had slicked-back hair, bright blue eyes, and a paunch belly that was moving under his shirt. Before we cleared him, his hand flashed out and grabbed my arm. I yelped and threw my elbow out at the guy. It slammed into his gut, and I felt the air whoosh out of his lungs. When he touched me, I knew he was the reason my internal radar was going crazy.

His looks were deceiving. He was Fae. And, I'd bet my house he worked for the queen. He didn't carry the same aura as the King's Guard.

My foot followed suit and crashed into his knee. I needed to get off the street, where I felt like a sitting duck. When I frantically glanced around, I spotted a massive church not too far away.

Letting go of Violet, I grabbed the Fae and pulled him with me. He wasn't going to let us pass without a fight, so I was going to give him one he'd never forget. As we got closer to the area, more humans were sight-seeing on the street out front.

I was committed to my path now, so I used the double-decker buses as cover and headed to the right of the massive building. Up close, it was one of the biggest, fanciest churches I'd ever seen. I snuck into the trees on the opposite side of the towers.

I was too confident in my hold and paid for the distraction. We weren't exactly hidden when his fist smacked into my face. My head snapped to the side, and I smashed it when I hit the ground.

"Fiona!" I didn't have time to ask Violet why she was shouting my name. I knew I needed to roll, or I was going to regret it. His booted foot came down, narrowly missing my chest.

Violet and Aislinn tossed spells at him while I pushed to my feet. Water flowed from his fingertips and hit Aislinn in the chest. I ran at him, but he kept pushing it at Aislinn while holding up a shield toward Violet. Some of her sparks made it around and hit him, making him grunt every time.

I heard many footsteps running down the sidewalk toward us from the direction of the main entrance. "I'm on it," Aislinn called out to me. I heard her cast a shield to hide us and turned my focus to the Fae. Just in time, too, because he had thrown a funnel of water at me.

It caught me, and I gasped a lungful of briny liquid. Coughing overtook me, making it impossible to hold my breath. My chest felt like a bonfire was burning in there. I couldn't say anything, but I focused on winds taking the water away and mouthed the word to cast the spell.

To my surprise, the wind blew against the water and whisked it away. Of course, I hadn't considered what would happen to me and ended up being tossed into a tree for my efforts. After hitting my back on the bark, I fell to the ground and braced myself when I landed. For the first time in longer than I could remember, my bad knee didn't threaten to make me throw up right then and there. In fact, I barely even felt the landing.

I had my shield up before he managed to start throwing a volley of spells my way. Standing up straight, I felt the phone vibrate in my back pocket, surprised it hadn't broken when I hit the tree.

"*Batto!*" I called out, keeping my focus on him. It was his turn to bounce around as my spell battered him over and over again.

The Fae's back was to Aislinn, and I could see more and more people coming to see what was going on. I didn't have time to stop and help. Thankfully, Violet joined her. I left them to deal with the humans.

"Violet keep searching for the kids," I called out, then followed that up with a spell. "*Glacio.*"

I watched ice spread over the Fae, but it never did what I wanted because he threw shards at me a second later. One impaled me a second later. Using elements against Fae and witches was risky because they wielded them easily.

My entire body hurt. I might be getting better, but I wasn't used to taking so much abuse. When a rock slams into my bad knee and sends me crashing to the grass, I react out of instinct.

"*Finis!*" I poured all of my intention toward him. I thought about what might be going through his head. Then about the blood pumping through his veins and the smug look on his face. It pissed me off and made me see red.

He relished hurting others. He didn't deserve to keep breathing. That wasn't very magnanimous of me, but I didn't care. Anyone who could take a life without hesitation was vile.

A smile broke out over my face when he went still. A second later, I lost the grin and gasped. I kept him pinned with my stare and couldn't miss the blank gaze looking back at me.

In the next second, electricity traveled all over my body. I shuddered with the feel of the massive influx of energy I received. All I could think was that I was drinking in his essence. The core of power in my belly that awoke when I moved to Pymm's Pondside swelled to overflowing. I was a sponge, taking it all in. My cells filled and plumped up, and I felt like I could fight a thousand enemies and run a marathon.

I went cold all over and fell to my knees, willing the connection to end. I had no desire to have any part of him inside me. There was nothing pure or clean about him. My stomach churned, and my gag reflex was trying to win a gold medal for the most pushups in under ten seconds.

The little bit of dinner I'd managed to eat came rushing back up and detoured to exit through my throat and nose. The connection was finally broken, and the influx stopped. My skin crawled, and my blood felt like sludge.

"I can't…" I couldn't catch my breath. Everything hurt, and I could feel the dark energy trying to merge with my own.

Violet was at my side. "What happened?"

"Oh, my Gods," Aislinn interrupted. "He's dead."

Violet's head snapped up, and her lower jaw dropped open. "Make sure the shield remains in place while I cleanse Fiona."

Aislinn said something I didn't catch while my stomach purged some more. This time what came up was black sludge. My vision wavered at that. I couldn't let this infect me. I would never be the same if I did.

Violet wrapped her arms around me and held me tightly. "*Purgo*." Her voice was soft, and I felt it more than I heard it. Bright white light washed through me. I felt the darkness recede with every inch it traveled until my vision cleared and my stomach stopped revolting.

I stood there gasping while I clung to Violet. I have no idea what happened just now, and I didn't have time to figure it out. "I'm okay. We need to find the kids now. Someone likely felt that expenditure of energy. You ready to get back to work?"

Violet's gaze ran over me from head to toe. She must have

seen what she was looking for because she nodded and turned to Aislinn. "They're to the West. I have no idea how far away they are, but it's definitely that direction. I think."

"Of course, they are. You have that super-duper momdar." Aislinn was teasing her, trying to alleviate her mood.

I sent a silent prayer to God that we were on the right track. I wanted to go home and crawl into bed and throw the covers over my head. It had been a long damn week already, and it wasn't over yet.

CHAPTER 14

"I swear I'm going to be covered in bruises. We really need to create a healing spell. Dark Fae assholes have no consideration for us middle-aged women." I rubbed the spot on my shoulder as we darted down the street.

We barely made it to the sidewalk, where a bunch of people were trying to see where the commotion was coming from when my skin started crawling. I tugged Violet's hand, and we slowed, trying to blend in with the others.

My eyes darted around the street as we walked to the left and the front of the cathedral. I gasped when I saw several small creatures scurrying out of the sewer. When one pair of beady green eyes landed on me, I tilted my head and kept glancing around at things like a tourist would.

"That building is so beautiful. We don't have much in the States with as much charm." My voice was too bright and obviously forced, but I needed to act normal, or they would follow us.

"What the hell are you talking about?" I grabbed Aislinn's

hand and squeezed it, giving her a go-with-me look. "Oh, you mean that building across the street?"

"Yeah. I mean, St. Paul's Cathedral is an icon in this city and for a good reason, but there is so much more." I lowered my voice and whispered, "Ugly little things coming from the sewer. Don't look. Let's keep going."

Violet's posture stiffened, but she pointed out the stained-glass windows close to us and told me some inane fact about them that didn't really register. It was far more complicated than I would have thought to keep my gaze from traveling back to the sewers and checking where the creatures were now.

By the time we made it to the end of the block, more appeared. This time they came from the direction we were heading. I recognized very few of them and couldn't ask anything at the moment.

One of them had a dozen arms and was seven feet tall. Another had pustules covering its grey face, and there was one with tentacles for eyes. They were terrifying. Thankfully, there was magic that shielded them from view, or chaos would break out in the middle of London.

There would be hundreds of panicked videos uploaded to the internet in a hot minute if others could see what was all around them. Instinct urged me to run. If I did that, I would draw attention. I'm certain I was shaking as I walked far too slowly for my liking.

It seemed like forever until we turned a corner, and I no longer caught sight of various creatures prowling through the shadows. "We need to get the hell out of here as fast as we can." My voice remained barely above a whisper, just in case.

Aislinn turned and glanced behind us, then blew out a breath. "Agreed. We can increase our pace a bit. We can't be walking too much longer. The river's going to stop our progress before long. We'll go back and get the car if we need to cross over.",

I pulled out my phone and shot a text to Sebastian letting him know we were heading toward the Thames from St. Paul Cathedral. He had to be getting close to us by now. Turns out it's tough to type and walk at the same time.

I stepped off the curb and nearly into traffic, twisted my ankle, and ran into a pole. How the heck does anyone do it so well? I guess if I was glued to my phone, I would have learned how to do everything and send a text like my children, but that has never been me.

Violet tugged my arm a few blocks away, and we changed directions slightly. "We need to turn here, then keep heading toward the river. My sense of them is getting stronger."

"It's about time something went our way." Aislinn wasn't wrong about that. It seemed like the deck was stacked against us lately. "Does anyone have a credit card or cash on them? I left my purse in the car, and I need a drink."

I patted my pockets and was about to tell her no when I pulled out my cell. "I keep forty bucks in my phone case. I started it years ago when I found myself in a situation with nothing but a phone, and I had to rely on my co-worker for a loan. The only problem is I haven't exchanged it for pounds yet, so we'd have to go somewhere that takes dollars."

"Thank the Gods you're prepared for just about anything. Loads of places take American money. Hey, is that Bas? And the sexy dragon?" Aislinn pointed to a car parked on the other side of the street.

I followed her finger and saw Sebastian glaring at us. A smile broke out over my face, and I crossed the street to join them. The river was on one side of us, and pubs, restaurants, and townhomes were on the other. Violet had stopped outside one of the pubs and was looking at the buildings around her. Aislinn paused in the middle of the road and turned back to Violet.

"Thanks for coming, Bas, Argies. Let's go over here. Violet may have homed in on the kids."

Bas grabbed my hand and twined our fingers together as he walked with me to Violet. With Argies on my left side, I felt sandwiched between hotness. I could smell Bas's sultry scent and Argies's spicy one over the Thames, which was a blessing.

I noticed Aislinn watching Argies and hoped things panned out between them. She needed something good in her life. I sucked at setting people up, so I hesitated in pushing him in her direction. I'd have to think on that one for a bit.

"Have you found them?" I called out to Violet.

She bit her lower lip before releasing it. "They're close. I feel them, but none of these rooflines looks like what I saw."

Argies continued walking down the sidewalk a few feet and paused about fifteen feet away. "There's a side street here. Did you check it?"

Violet shook her head and was moving in the blink of an eye. "I haven't been that far."

I was right behind her, wishing I could do more to help her at this point. When I tried to extract my hand from Sebastian's, he refused to let go. I cocked an eyebrow at him and got a scowl in return.

I was about to tease him when Violet cried out. This time I took off running and was at her side in an instant. "What is it?"

Violet was staring at a set of about five townhouses connected to one another. "They're in there. And they're still alive. Let's go."

Sebastian stopped Violet with a hand on her shoulder. "Wait. We can't just rush through the doors without doing some reconnaissance. We risk their lives if we aren't prepared to handle whatever is in there."

Violet's eyes filled with tears and her shoulders slumped. "I can't stand that they are so close, and yet I can't rescue them. I know you're right, but I don't like it. I want to blow something up."

Aislinn wrapped an arm over her shoulder and held her. "Save it for the mission. And I think it's a safe bet the Backside of Forty will be blowing something up before the night is through."

Argies chuckled and shook his head side to side. "I've never met women so bloodthirsty as you three."

I lifted a shoulder. "Then you've never met a mother whose babies were in danger. Fuck with our kids or us, and you get burned."

"Mainly because you can't control your fire," Violet teased me. It was good to see she was still in there. I know this situation was killing her. She'd been the mother and father to her kids for years since her ex-husband left her for a younger woman. He was a Disneyland dad, taking the kids to do fun stuff every few weekends. But he was never there for the critical events. And never backed her up with discipline.

Sebastian nudged my shoulder. "Butterfly's magic might be chaotic, but it packs a punch. We're lucky to have her on our team. I wasn't so sure at first, but she proved my assumption wrong."

Argies smiled. "Bas wrong? The realms must have collided, and I'm in a coma from the resulting explosion. This is all a dream, isn't it?"

Bas growled while Aislinn laughed. "That's a good one. I never imagined I'd hear those words come out of his mouth. But, let's not tempt Fate with world-ending jokes."

Violet shook her head and pointed to the opposite side of the street. "There's a café here. Let's grab a table while we watch the comings and goings, so we can get to the saving already."

"Great idea. Do they take dollars?" I scanned the plate glass window and door but didn't see any indication.

"I've got the bill. Where is your car?" Sebastian asked as he scanned the area.

"That's over by St. James park. We were headed to the market there and ran into a witch that I shut up, then some imps crawled through some portal, and we took off running." I started to walk to the café, and everyone followed.

Bas was growling again. "How the hell did someone travel in this dimension? And, how is it that you attract so many Fae to you?"

I held up my hands and paused outside the door. "It's not my fault. They crawled out of some kind of portal, and that one at St. Paul's Cathedral grabbed me, so I killed him."

"And then you had to purge black bile from inhaling his dark magic."

Bas had opened the door and glanced back at me with wide eyes. A couple left the restaurant and moved around us. We remained quiet while we went inside and were seated at a table in the far corner, next to the window.

A waiter took our drink order and gave us a few minutes to look over the menu. Bas didn't even pick his up. "You inhaled his essence? Do you have a death wish? Or are you eager to jump sides?"

My ire was up now. "You need to watch your tone. First, I did nothing to take his energy inside me. I fought it every second of the way. My stomach still hurts from throwing up that black goo. If there is a way to keep that from happening, I'd appreciate being told. I haven't had time to read as much as I would have. It's been non-stop bullshit for over a week now."

Sebastian looked at me with narrowed eyes. "That charm should have protected you."

I pulled it out from under my shirt. "I think it broke when I was pulled through the portal."

"Fuck. I'll do another spell when we return home. The gem needs to be restored, or it will dissipate." Bas had never offered to give me anything before, and it left me speechless.

The waiter came and took our order. The Shepherd's pie was calling my name. Light flashed outside, and I gasped when I noticed a green glow emanating from the townhouse on the end.

"What is that?" I wondered if one of the kids tried to escape and activated it.

"I think it's an alarm of sorts," Argies interjected. "I saw movement in the lower left-hand window right before it lit up."

Several men came running down the block. I also noticed movement on the upper floors. "Are those shifters or elves? I can't see their ears."

"Likely both. They're Dark Fae. You see how black their auras are?" Bas ran a hand over his jaw as he watched the commotion.

The light went out the second they entered the house. There was a split second while the door was open when I got a glimpse of some imps and a big black dog inside the house.

"Did anyone see what rune they used when they deactivated the alarm?" Bas directed his question to the entire table and didn't bother keeping his voice down. I guess he didn't really say anything that would cause attention.

"It was a common disarming rune," Argies interjected. "They have backup nearby, so we will have to keep one of us at the front door."

I shook my head. "We should stay together. It's never good to separate when you go into a situation like this."

Sebastian placed his hand over mine. "You're right about that. You three will remain together. Ever since you formed your coven and shared power, you are all stronger when you have each other. Argies and I can handle ourselves."

Argies bobbed his head in agreement. Men! I scowled at them both. "There's no need to be cavemen. We will head downstairs as a group. We can face anything that attacks as a unit."

"Splitting their focus will give us an advantage. You never allow them to have all of their power players in the same place at the same time. Argies and I will throw some spells that display our power and get them to divide their forces."

Argies took a drink then set his cup down. "Can you arrange to have your car taken home? It'll be easier if we all leave in Sebastian's truck. The more time we spend here, the more likely someone will capture one of us."

Violet sat forward. "We have to go now. I think they're hurting one of the kids."

We all lowered our gaze. "Are you sure? We will be taking a chance one or more of us will be killed. There are easily a couple dozen in there now." I hated that I didn't jump up and race across the street, but I had to be smart about this. More than Ben and Bailey depended on us being successful here.

Violet turned red-rimmed eyes my way. "I feel her pain. What if they kill her? It's tearing me up inside. I won't survive losing them."

I clasped her hands in mine. "I promise you we will not let that happen. I think we wait until the ones that just arrived leave. It's our best option. Can you send them any messages? If they know we are here, they will do everything they need to survive."

"Do you think they can sense you, too? Maybe that's why they set off that alarm. They might want to alert you or try to escape and find you." Aislinn had a point. Those kids loved their mother. It seemed highly likely that they knew she was close.

Violet wiped a tear from her cheek. "You're right. The connection goes both ways. I bet Bailey knows I'm here for sure."

"That's great. Let her know we will be in there soon. What wall did you see them chained to?"

Violet closed her eyes and muttered the melding spell under her breath. "They're on the outside wall, I think."

"Before we go in, we need a plan to cast a protective bubble around that area. I don't want any of the assholes in there to try and take them out while we infiltrate their location. If we do it from outside, will it cover the right area?"

Bas looked over at Argies, who nodded. "I'm going to take care of that right now. I can go in unseen and push a rune through the wall to them. That way, they won't be hurt anymore."

Aislinn laid her hand over his and squeezed. "Thank you. I wasn't sure how much longer I could wait. My heart is going to give out with how fast it's beating."

"Mine, too," I agreed.

Violet sniffed and wiped her eyes again. "You're a good dragon, Argies. Thank you."

He inclined his head and got up from the table. We watched him walk out the door. I didn't see where he went, but I had my eyes trained on that side of the house and saw blue light flash then disappear. My heart didn't slow down at all, but my gut unknotted.

The waitress delivered our food then, and I took a couple bites while we waited for the latest guards to leave. If they didn't exist soon, I was heading over anyway. The twins were protected, and we needed to get them the hell out of there.

CHAPTER 15

"They know we're here. They felt the protection slip around them. But it could have alerted the guards about us, as well. I'm not getting many clear images, but I saw one of them strike out at Ben as he was in between Bailey and an asshole with grey skin and too many eyes that were looking at her in ways that made me want to vomit," Violet croaked out as she held a hand over her stomach.

"At least the dragon did something right." Bas had his usual scowl as he paid the bill. We declined boxes to take the mostly uneaten food with us. I was acutely aware of Sebastian's presence since he kept his hand at the small of my back while we left the restaurant.

Out on the sidewalk, he guided us in the opposite direction. "We need to wait for the new arrivals to leave. It would be foolish to attack while they're on high alert." Bas placed his hands on my shoulders.

"For once, I agree with Sebastian," Argies said as he approached us from the opposite side of the street. I had no idea how he moved so fast. "They sensed something after I cast the spell and immediately jumped into action like a hive of bees."

Violet cried out and covered her mouth before darting her gaze to the house in question then back at us. "We shouldn't have taken the chance. Now they won't stop until they kill them."

I grabbed hold of her shoulders and looked into her eyes. "Stop that. They're protected, and we will get in there before they do anything to harm them." Pedestrians strolled along the streets, chatting happily. Their contentment tried to lull me into a sense of calm at the same time adrenaline was racing through my system in preparation for battle.

Aislinn nodded and squeezed Violet's hand. "Besides, I'd bet those idiots assumed it was the kids that cast the spell. They aren't the smartest bunch, and if they suspected we were outside, they would have rushed out in search of Argies."

That was a good point. Argies managed to sneak right up to the building without alerting anyone to his presence outside. It was surprising they didn't have some kind of perimeter spell. Then again, it was located in a high traffic area. I could only hope they got a lot of false alarms for the same reasons. That would make their response time slower.

I dropped my hands from Violet and turned to Argies. "Did you see anything else we should be prepared for when you got close to the house?"

Argies pursed his lips. "The windows are blocked by magic, so no one can see inside. I couldn't confirm how many are inside, but I sensed more energy from the main and upper floors."

Bas twined our hands together and tugged me down the street. Once again, we were moving away from the house. "You three will join me, and we will go in the back door while Argies kicks in the front. The distraction should give you three the perfect window to head downstairs."

We stopped in front of a coffee shop, and Aislinn snagged Argies's forearm. "Sounds like a plan. Let's grab a drink, so we don't raise suspicion."

I glanced up and made a note of the cute storefront. There was a bay window with the name of the place painted in gold over it. The storefront and trim were all black. I inhaled the heavenly scent of roasted coffee beans the second the door opened. It had been months since I'd gone into a place that primarily sold coffee. It brought back nostalgia as I recalled all my visits before shifts at the hospital.

I didn't order anything. I was too nervous, but Argies looked at me. "I believe you mentioned something about caffeinated beverages while you were complaining about what we had to offer to in Eidothea, so what do you recommend."

I chuckled and bobbed my head. "You have got to try a white mocha latte. If you're here next month when everything pumpkin spice comes out, you should try a pumpkin spice latte. I personally can't stand the seasonal flavor. I'm a chocolate girl through and through."

Aislinn gasped. "I'm not sure we can be friends anymore. I wish I'd known sooner."

I smacked her shoulder. "Good thing I love you for who you are and don't hold your love of pumpkin spice against you."

Violet, who had been smiling with us, lost her amusement and walked to the front window. "They're leaving."

The barista called out our order at that moment. Aislinn and I hurried to the counter and grabbed the cups. Violet held hers close to her chest while Argies sipped his. We were halfway out the door when the dragon shifter moaned rather loudly.

I shot him wide eyes embarrassed that the sound had my body reacting as if I was a teenager again. Aislinn groaned and moved closer to him. Even Violet shuddered. When a hand landed on my lower hip, I glanced over and met Bas's gaze. It was clear he was upset, but he always was, so I had no idea why he seemed angrier at the moment.

I liked to think it was because he was jealous and wanted me for himself. *Delusional much? He hasn't yet laid eyes on your mom bod.* The heat in his eyes did an excellent job of helping me shove aside all of the doubt I still harbored.

It had been over two decades since I was with a man other than my husband. I haven't had guilt about being with someone else. I've had enough time since Tim died to understand I am not cheating on him, but I am not dead either. What I hadn't given much thought to until the last few months was how I look.

My body carried my story in all its imperfect glory. My stomach and breasts show evidence of how far my skin stretched to accommodate my babies. My hips, too, for that matter. No one had seen the dimpled wonderland below my saggy ass.

Before I could move back to the essential matters, Bas grabbed me and planted a quick kiss on my mouth. The kiss set my panties on fire and had me salivating for more. He felt the same way, according to the erection pressing against my stomach anyway.

Shaking my head, I forced my eyes away from his heated ones. I hoped we would explore that more later. After we were all home safe. The kids needed us. As I focused down the street, my heart took off like a shot. Ten guards had left the house and were turning the corner and out of our line of sight.

My body was bristling with unfulfilled desire, so I started down the street with the rest behind me. Aislinn teased Bas as we walked. "You know biting her would leave a visible mark no one could ignore. Then you wouldn't have random guys flirting with her."

I held up my hand. "Don't even think about it. I will geld you if you try it. I decide who bites me and where."

"It's just a matter of time before you beg me to place my mark on you," Sebastian promised.

When we reached the row of houses, Argies squeezed Aislinn's hand before we separated, and he disappeared in the shadows. How the hell did he do that? He wasn't using magic. I didn't feel any fluctuations around us—question one million for another time.

Sebastian was a looming figure that I was sure the neighbors would see out their back windows. I regretted the jeans the second we reached the wood fence separating the small yards.

Aislinn was up and over while Violet and I shared a look. "Perhaps..ahhh!" The shout left me when Bas lifted me and practically tossed me over to the other side. I twisted and grabbed the top so I didn't fall and break something. It wasn't far to the ground, and I let myself drop right as Violet was being placed over it, as well.

Within seconds Sebastian was standing beside me, and Violet was dropping down. The flowers in the pots filling this yard scented heavily in the air. We were all up and into the yard of the house in question a couple minutes later. None of the residents going about their evening heard us or came out to investigate.

When I landed on the grass, I found Aislinn fighting one of the creatures that had tentacles. She kicked and threw punches while dodging balls of light. I raced to help her and got hit in the left shoulder by a spell before I managed to do anything. The loud crack of energy should have alerted someone around us, but I didn't hear anyone responding.

The smell of ozone followed a second later, making me wonder if it was the magic or something else.

Sebastian snuck up beside us, silent as the night, and snapped the thing's neck. I gaped at him and watched as he dropped the body and continued to the back door. He traced a rune above the lock and pushed the door open. His subsequent movements were fast as lightning.

Violet, Aislinn, and I raced through next and found ourselves in the kitchen of the townhome. The smell of rotting trees hit me next slammed into like a fist. It was enough to almost knock me on my ass. The space was small, and the attached dining room was empty. There was nothing on the walls except green blood. At least it looked better than red.

A scan of the nearby living room revealed no furniture either. We needed to find the basement. There were two doors on the other side of the refrigerator. The first one showed a pantry and the second one revealed a set of stairs. I paused before going down to make sure no one needed our help.

Sebastian was at the open pass that lead to the other section of the house fighting four creatures. I hear shouting from the front door but couldn't see Argies. They could handle themselves. My friends were heading into the unknown and would need me.

The staircase was a death trap, narrow and steep. Violet and Aislinn were throwing spells when I reached the bottom. There were two Fae between the kids and us. "You get around them while Aislinn and I keep them busy," I told Violet as I added a fireball. The crackle of flames in my palm was almost as satisfying as the loud snap when it hit the wall. The Fae in front of me had managed to jump away. Thankfully, it created an opening for Violet to get by.

She took off, and I called up another ball of flames. The

first one had ended up hitting the shield around Ben and Bailey and falling to the floor. If that had been a wood floor or had the usual debris you'd find in a basement, I would have started a fire. Thankfully, we were surrounded by stone. Still, I'd need to be careful. Not my strong suit when it came to my magic.

I replayed all the spells I'd learned and tossed out spells to bludgeon the Fae. I was getting used to feeling the power build in my body and exit through my fingertips. I tossed one high, making his head snap back while the other hand threw one low, making his knee buckle.

Blue sparks left his hand, and I twisted out of the way, avoiding the blow. I heard Violet talking to Ben and Bailey but tuned them out. I needed to focus. The wind started up from one of the Fae. It tossed Aislinn into me. We grabbed each other, and I tried to keep us from landing on our asses.

I screamed out a warning to Violet right before my hip hit the hard floor. Aislinn bounced off my curves a split second later, and Violet turned from the kids. As I anticipated, the Fae both went after her.

I shouted, "*Ferio*," and threw both hands toward the guards. Their bodies jerked and flew toward Violet, who added one of her own. Pounding footsteps echoed behind us, and I twisted my head to see clawed feet coming toward us.

I didn't have time to move before I was hit with electricity. It sizzled through my body. My back arched and I twitched. Agony trailed as the worst aftereffect on the planet. The smell of burning hair made it all the worse. My stomach revolted while I writhed in pain.

One of the tentacled Fae grabbed a fistful of my hair and pulled me up while a lizard-like one took hold of Aislinn's arm. I heard a crack followed by her scream. Rather than deal with the one dragging me, I had to help Aislinn.

A bone was poking at her shoulder in a way that told me

she was a thin membrane away from a compound fracture. "*Infineon!*" Both of my hands waved at Aislinn's attacker. I made sure to add my desire to have this one cut to ribbons. I was over-killing one of the creatures. My friends were in danger, and I wasn't leaving one of them alive to hurt someone I love.

Dark green blood spurted as an arm went flying. A leg was next, and its head detached going one direction while its body fell in another. Aislinn's arm hung limply at her side, but she flung water at an approaching tentacled fiend.

Ben, Bailey, and Violet joined us, and the four of us faced off with the three Fae that were standing in the way of our exit. The one in the middle was the many-eyed man with grey skin. "Petra!" Small stones flew from my hands and into the grotesque eyeballs staring at us. The wet pop as the eyes ruptured made me want to fist pump the air until the smell of dead fish hit me.

"Help Aislinn and make sure they don't reach you," Violet told her kids. They listened immediately, closing the distance. Bailey wrapped an arm around Aislinn while Ben kicked the bodies out of our way so we didn't trip.

"You messed with the wrong witch's kids, asshole." Violet balled her hands into fists at her sides.

I was tossing fire at the one closest to me when I heard Violet's shout. "*Ensis!*"

I turned, expecting to see a steel sword, and was surprised to see a blue glow in Violet's hands. It was almost like a lightsaber, except it didn't have a rounded blade or solid shape.

She swung, and a loud swoosh preceded wind blowing my hair back. She had a wicked follow-through. I watched her push through some resistance before an audible snick. She had cut off fingers.

A fist slammed into the side of my skull while I watched

her swing her spelled blade back and forth. I threw a punch while I ducked, hoping to hit the thing's groin. Surely, all beings had the same weakness.

I wasn't sure if they had genitals because I connected with a high. One that was solid enough to bruise my knuckles. I was sucking air and tired enough to pass out. One more piece of shit, and we could get out of here.

Or not. Footsteps sounded on the stairs, urging me to finish this shit. I used the same spell as Violet just had and swung as fast as I could. Limbs and chunks of gray flesh went flying.

My chest was heaving, and I was covered in brackish blood, but I was ready when two sets of boots hit the bottom of the stairs. I lifted the blade, prepared to take the next on but released the spell and sagged where I stood.

"Aislinn's hurt badly. Carry her, and let's get the hell out of here," I instructed Sebastian. He scanned me from head to toe before nodding and turning to pick Aislinn up.

"I've got her. Let's get out of here before more arrive." Argies had moved to Aislinn's side before I managed to say anything to Bas. The dragon cradled her close to his chest and brushed the hair off her forehead.

"You okay?" I asked Violet.

"I'm done with this fucking day, but we're all alive."

I nodded in agreement and climbed the stairs groaning when the ache in my hips reminded me of the fall that I took a bit ago. Sebastian was at my side and wrapped his arm around my waist when we reached the kitchen.

The cool night air brushed over my heated skin, and I barely registered when he nudged me across the street close to the café we'd eaten at earlier in the evening. I saw why when several of the guards ran down the road to the house.

"That was close," Ben said behind me.

Too close for comfort. "We did it. I can't believe we pulled that off."

Sebastian looked at me with one eyebrow lifted. "You need more faith in yourself. You guys fought as many as we did upstairs. Not many can claim that."

I smirked at him. "That's because the Backside of Forty kick ass. Does anyone have a portal to Pymm's Pondside? I need a damn shower, and Aislinn needs a doctor."

"I've already sent a message to Zreegy. She'll be at your house by the time we get there," Violet replied as we all climbed into Bas's truck.

I sank into the seat and closed my eyes when he pulled onto the road. I felt like I could take a beat and relax for the first time in a week. Ben and Bailey were safe, and we were on our way home. There was still an evil asshole to find and deal with, but for the moment, I could sleep.

CHAPTER 16

"*H*ow are they?" Violet practically pounced on Zreegy the second she descended the stairs. It had taken all of my best friend's willpower to obey the healer's edict and remain downstairs while she looked over her kids.

Ben and Bailey clung to their mother the entire ride back. Both had bruises marring their faces, but Ben favored his left side and had everyone worried.

Zreegy put the stethoscope into her bag and zipped it closed. "Bailey is shaken and has some significant bruising along with a minor concussion. Ben suffered the worst of it. I suspect he stood between the elves and his sister. He has three broken ribs and a bruised liver. I suspect his kidney might be injured, as well, so you need to keep an eye on him."

Tears sprang to Violet's eyes, and I enveloped her in a hug. Aislinn wrapped her arms around Violet from the other side. "Should we take them to the hospital?"

Zreegy shook her head. "Not at this point. Tonight will be a long one for them, but they will be feeling much better by tomorrow afternoon. It will be a couple days before Ben is completely out of the woods. I know this is difficult, but remember they heal far faster than a human." The healer turned to Aislinn. "You need to keep your arm in the sling for a few days and ice it for twenty minutes every couple of hours. You did a number on it, but it will heal."

I shivered when Zreegy pinned me with her stare. "You know how to watch for signs of internal bleeding, correct?"

My heart settled, and I swallowed the lump that had formed in my throat. This was familiar territory for me. I bobbed my head and squeezed Violet tighter when she made a noise of alarm. "I do. I'll make sure they get to the hospital if I suspect anything is off."

"There are no signs either of them is bleeding at this point, but we both know trauma. If you weren't here, I would be staying until morning just to be safe. I'm glad you can do more than just guard the portal." Zreegy turned to leave and stopped when my Grams stood there glaring at her.

"As if guarding the portal isn't enough. This town has always been ungrateful for the job that has always fallen to a Shakleton. You should be bowing at Fiona's feet."

I released my friend and crossed to Grams' side. "No, she shouldn't, Grams. You were the only Guardian for decades, and Zreegy has been the only healer here for even longer. It's not easy having no one to help. You know that better than anyone. Everyone here appreciates what you dedicated your life to. And, they miss having you here."

"Hmmm." Was the only reply from Grams.

"I will be available if anything happens." With that proclamation, Zreegy left through the front door.

Violet glanced at the ceiling. "I don't want to take them back to the house. They were supposed to be safe, and instead, our enemies breached my protections and took my kids."

"You guys will stay here as long as you need. There are plenty of rooms." I almost didn't offer Violet a place to stay. After all, my house had been the sight of more than one fight recently. But, in the end, I knew the energy we'd poured into securing the land meant this was now one of the safest places in Cottlehill Wilds.

"My place is always open, as well," Aislinn offered. "I might have the best views in town, but my place is much smaller, and I don't have the wards like we put here at Pymm's Pondside."

"I love your place. Being so close to the ocean has always calmed me," Violet admitted, "but it's best if we stay here. Maybe you should stay here for a couple days, too. You live all alone on the cliffs. With the rest of us unreachable, you might become the next target."

Aislinn glanced at Argies but quickly shifted her gaze around the rest of the room. I couldn't help but notice the way her cheeks turned pink. I think my friend had the hots for the dragon.

"I'm not going anywhere. The Backside of Forty is far stronger together. I just need to grab some clothes."

"Can you get some things for me from the house, as well?" Bailey's voice had everyone turning to the stairs as she and Ben came down.

Violet rushed to their side. "How are you feeling? Can I get you some tea or anything?"

Bailey's lower lip trembled for a second before she nodded and grabbed her mom's hand. "Tea and maybe some scones, if there are any."

Of all the times not to have much in the house. "I don't have scones, but I do have some cookies."

Sebastian uncrossed his arms. "I'll run to the store to grab some basics. I can even pick up whatever you need from your house."

Bailey chewed on her lower lip, but I interjected before

she had to embarrass herself. No woman wanted to have a man rifling through her drawers. "Why don't you take Aislinn, and she can help gather Bailey's stuff?"

"I'm going too. If anyone tries to attack, it will be better to have two of us." Argies was looking at Aislinn when he spoke, and it made me wonder if he was just as into her.

Ever since I met him, Argies had indicated an interest in me. I was flattered. I'd never really had many men interested in me, and for a minute, it felt good to be seen as desirable. I had a mom body with stretch marks, saggy boobs, extra weight, and love handles.

I'd been reluctant to consider my love interests much beyond enjoying the attention of two hot guys. Still, I was glad to see him possibly showing an interest in my friend. Aislinn deserved someone as wonderful as Argies. Besides, I couldn't deny Sebastian was the one for me.

I didn't think I was ready for anything too serious, but I wasn't going to deny where my heart was either. I still had far more important shit going on in my life. I was a middle-aged woman capable of multitasking and not losing sight of what was most urgent because some sexy guy smiled at me. I couldn't have said the same when I was in my twenties. After all, that was how I ended up married and pregnant before I finished nursing school.

"Don't forget to pick up some fruit and sandwich stuff while you're shopping. We will have a full house, and Fiona hasn't gone grocery shopping in far too long." Grams floated into the kitchen, and we watched as she stuck her head through the refrigerator and pantry doors, reciting a list of what Bas should get from the store.

"Grams. Sebastian is perfectly capable of getting food. Besides, he doesn't need to get much. I will go out tomorrow and stock up." I almost amended that statement and asked for a few things. I was all out of wine and tequila. I had some scotch and vodka, but not much.

Ben told Aislinn what he wanted, as did Violet, and then the trio left through the backdoor. Violet led the kids to the couch, and I put the kettle on for tea. I was terrible at making the stuff, according to Grams. In England, it was an art form that I had yet to master.

I added the usual suspects to a tray, poured the hot water into the pot with the leaves, and then carried it into the living room. After setting it down, I crossed to the fireplace and set logs on the grates.

When I reached for the matches, Grams floated in front of me. "Use your magic to light the fire."

I blinked and looked up at her. There wasn't a moment I forgot I had magic, but I wasn't used to using it for anything but fighting. Sure, I'd done simple spells like tracking and protections, but it always concerned some emergency or another. It's funny that I never considered using magic for everyday things because that had been what I was most excited about when I discovered I was a witch.

"Alright." Focusing on the wood and kindling, I called up the power bubbling in my chest. "*Ignis*." A second after uttering the spell, flames shot out of the grate and had me stumbling onto my ass.

Violet chuckled as she set the teapot down after pouring each of us a cup. "I think you're still amped up."

"Good thing the house is fire resistant," Grams grumbled.

"I'm still learning how much energy to pour into spells. It seems I either dump everything I have into them or nothing at all." I swore I was going to master this shit eventually. I was used to learning things quickly, so the fact that I still felt like I didn't know anything irritated me to no end.

"It's all about balancing your emotions," Bailey inter-jected, surprising us all. Violet beamed at her daughter. "Fear drives you but can also block your power. Anger too, but in different ways. And panic can make you freeze up entirely."

Ben slid closer to his sister, wincing as he moved. "Anyone in our shoes would have panicked. Countless dark elves were coming after us."

Violet's smile vanished and was replaced by a furrowed brow. "None of this is your fault, sweetie."

Tears slipped past Bailey's lower lashes to stream down her face. "But it is. I'm the one that let them through the door. If I had kept my head, I could have helped Ben reinforce the wards when they started pounding on the boundary."

Ben tried to lift his arm and wrap it around his sister, but he didn't get very far. Bailey's tears increased when he gasped in obvious pain. Violet already had her daughter wrapped in her embrace.

I knelt in front of Ben. "Broken ribs are brutal. You didn't feel any stabbing pain just now, did you?" I needed to make sure the bones didn't shift and cause more damage. He shook his head.

I lifted a hand to examine him and stopped. I didn't want to add to his pain. Realizing I could use my magic, I called up a spell. I wasn't a healer like Zreegy, but I knew anatomy. "*Exploro*," I muttered under my breath.

At first, nothing happened, and I realized I wasn't adding my intent for the spell. It was important that Ben hadn't done something, like puncture a lung when he moved. I kept thoughts of his body and injuries, plus the need to know if anything vital was damaged at the front of my mind.

In my mind's eye, I detected the broken ribs. I'd need to tape them to help stabilize the area. Zreegy was right, his kidney was damaged along with his liver, but his spleen was as well. I didn't see any active bleeding, but I would be rechecking him in an hour. Splenectomies were common in

157

trauma cases. I didn't want to miss if Ben's condition worsened.

Several seconds later, I released the breath I had been holding and opened my eyes to see Violet and Bailey staring at me. "Is he okay?" They blurted in unison.

I smiled at them and climbed to my feet. "He's not worse. I'm going to tape his ribs so they don't shift and injure his lung. You need to take it easy, Ben. And I mean it. There isn't internal bleeding, but if you don't rest, it will change quickly, and you might even need surgery."

I headed to the bathroom, where Grams was waiting for me. "Your power is growing faster than I expected. You shouldn't have been able to see inside his body like that. You will need to share more of your power with your friends."

"Is that safe for them? I already made Violet a target that endangered her kids. I don't want them in even more danger."

Grams' silver hair was loose over her shoulders like she usually wore it and glinted in the fluorescent light as she shook her head from side to side. "You have no choice. And if you asked them, they would demand you do it. You have changed them already anyway. They are no longer what they were. Their power is greater thanks to you."

I whirled on my grandmother, nearly dropping the white tape from my first aid kit. "Why didn't you tell me sharing with them was going to alter them in such a way? I never would have done it."

"Which is precisely why I didn't tell you. You had no choice, Fiona. And your friends knew the risk, yet they agreed anyway. You are rare. I knew when you were a young child, you were special. So did your parents. We just didn't know you were the unicorn of witches."

I wanted to rant and rail at my Grams, but it would do no

good. What was done was done. "They have more power now, too?"

Grams nodded. "They do. You've given them a priceless gift. They can now do things they never could have imagined. The three of you together are a force never before seen."

Part of me wanted to take it back and relieve my friends of the burden, but the selfish part of me was glad I wasn't in this alone. I needed my girls at my side to get through whatever was to come. Shoving those thoughts aside, I returned to the living room right as Bas, Aislinn, and Argies returned.

"Alright, Ben. This is going to hurt. I can cast a spell to dull the pain."

"I'd prefer a glass of scotch or whiskey if you have it. My nerves are still on edge, and it will help." He turned pleading eyes to his mother. He and Bailey weren't technically old enough to drink, but it seemed to me they were close enough. That decision, however, was up to their mother.

Violet sighed and got up from the couch. "Alright, but just one drink. I could use a glass of wine, as well."

"I don't have any. We drank the last of it the other night."

Aislinn held up a bag. "I grabbed some when we were out."

"You are a lifesaver," I told her with a smile before turning to Ben. "I'm going to take your shirt off. Don't lift your left arm. We don't want you shifting those bones." I was careful as I tugged the fabric over his head but couldn't keep from causing him pain.

Violet hovered behind me as I wrapped the wide tape around his chest. The area was already purple and definitely swollen. I could feel my best friend's anger behind me. I wanted to reassure her everything had turned out alright, but I wanted the blood of whoever was responsible as much as she did.

"I swear when we find out who was behind this, I am going to rip their arms from their sockets and beat them with it," Aislinn growled.

I glanced at my blood-thirsty friend. "You will make a fierce mama bear one day."

She snorted. "Not likely. I'm almost forty and single. Kids just aren't an option for me anymore."

"That's not true, Aunt Aislinn. You're still plenty young to have kids. You'd make a great mom," Bailey said, surprising us.

"Thank you, Bailey, but there is still the problem of being single. I don't see that changing anytime soon. And, even if it did, I would need to find a guy I liked for more than two seconds."

Argies tilted his head and considered her words. "Are you afraid of commitment?"

"Nope. I'm not afraid of it at all. What I'm unwilling to do is saddle myself with another asshole. In my experience, very few men are capable of true love and loyalty." I understood what she was saying and would likely feel the same way if I had an ex like hers.

Bodin was married to Aislinn for over ten years and was cheating on her the entire time. She discovered his infidelity when his latest girlfriend ended up pregnant with his baby. It was a massive scandal in Cottlehill Wilds because the woman used to work for Violet and was friends with the two of them. As if that wasn't enough to make you hate men, Violet's husband ran off with a young nymph, as well. It was no surprise the two of them refused to consider dating.

"I don't need details to know someone hurt you badly," Argies told her with an intense look. "Whoever it was is an idiot. If I had a woman like you, I wouldn't be able to think of anyone else. Judging all men based on a few bad ones limits your options, and ultimately you will end up alone. You deserve more than to allow some asshole to rob you of your future happiness."

Violet sat forward. "I never thought of it like that."

Ben was gritting his teeth, and sweat dotted his forehead as I finished securing his ribs. "He's right, mom. You shouldn't let dad ruin the rest of your life."

Violet smiled at her son. "You shouldn't talk about your dad like that."

Bailey huffed and crossed her arms over her chest. "Why not, mom? He treated you like shit. And he was always yelling at us. He wasn't a good dad or husband."

I set the tape down and clapped my hands. "How about that wine?" We all needed to relax and put the night behind us. The situation was far from over, but at the moment, we all needed a beat to recuperate so we could fight another day.

CHAPTER 17

*A*n alarm slid through me, making me catch my breath. The warning came from Pymm's Pondside, telling me someone had crossed onto the property. The magic didn't sense malevolent intentions, which is the only reason they were able to cross. That didn't mean my visitor had my best interest in mind.

"What is it?" Sebastian's voice carried his usual demand. Thankfully I was a grown-ass woman with no desire to follow anyone blindly, or I'd be falling all over myself to respond.

He's only asking because he wants to be prepared to defend you. The reminder was enough for me to ignore my stubborn side. "Someone entered the property."

"Friend or foe?"

Violet's question followed right after Sebastian's follow-up. "Could it be Tunsall?"

Knocking on the front door answered Violet's inquiry, but nothing else. I tuned into everything around me like Grams had been telling me to do. I was glad to have the book but far more grateful to have my grandmother and her snarky direction. I'd learned how to hone the skills I'd mastered and was picking up new ones.

Getting up, I was acutely aware of Sebastian following me to the door and my Grams chastising him for not allowing me to flex my magical muscle. I didn't need to turn around to know the corner of his right eye would be twitching, and his jaw clenched to keep his mouth shut.

A smile hovered at the corner of my mouth until I opened the door and saw Lance standing on my stoop. Why the hell was the Chief Constable here? My gut twisted into knots. My closest friends and family were in the house safe and sound, but that didn't make me feel too much better. His presence could only mean the killer had struck again.

"Constable. What can I do for you?"

Lance's brown eyes looked down on me. His face held a grim expression. It was the same as I had seen each time I'd spoken to the man. "I need to talk to you about Kendra Williams."

I tilted my head. "Who?" The name didn't ring any bells.

"May I?" The Constable looked beyond me to Sebastian standing at my back.

I turned my head and noticed Violet and Aislinn telling my grandmother to hide. The very human police officer would not understand why he saw a ghost in the form of my dead Grams.

Turning, I stepped back and gestured inside the house. "Sure. 'C'mon in."

Violet strode into view. "We were just sitting down for a cuppa. Can I get you one?"

"I'd appreciate it. I've got a long day ahead of me." Lance continued through my house, following in Violet's wake.

I still didn't understand the obsession the English had

with tea. Coffee was a far better choice. Of course, they felt the same about Americans and java. I paused before entering the kitchen and leaned into Bas.

"Do you know Kendra Williams? Or what this is about?"

Sebastian shook his head from side to side while keeping his gaze trained on the other room. "No idea, but it's not good. We need to tweak the wards to keep him out."

"That would be difficult to explain." I patted his broad chest and continued to the island where Violet was pouring tea into a mug for Lance.

"You mentioned someone named Kendra Williams, but I don't know her. What is this about?" I tucked my hands behind my back to hide the way they shook.

Lance took a sip and set the mug down. "Ms. Williams was attacked this morning in the park. She would be dead right now if Mae hadn't discovered her and called for help."

I couldn't stop my eyes from flaring or my mouth from dropping open. "That's awful, but what does this have to do with me?" And why did Mae call the human authorities for help?

Lance pursed his lips as Aislinn and Argies entered the room. For several tense seconds, I didn't think he would respond while they were present. He broke his silence right when I was about to ask them to leave. "She was carrying your picture and a gun. What do you know about that?"

"I have no idea. Like I said before. I don't know who this person is and certainly can't say why she would be carrying my picture." I had seen enough TV shows about cops and investigations to know I was a suspect. "I haven't left my house since returning with Ben and Bailey from London last night around ten."

"We were all together the entire evening, so if you think she might have done something, you're wrong…" Sebastian's deep voice sent shivers through me. It was, in large part, how turned on I was hearing him defend me. We'd been dancing around each other for months. It was getting hard to deny how badly I wanted to throw caution to the wind and take him to my bed.

Lance rested his fisted hands on the counter as he leaned forward. "I'm looking at every piece of evidence we have been able to gather. It seems she was attacked shortly before four this morning, and the only clue we have is your picture."

Bas crossed his arms over his chest. "Go ask her why she had it with her. Fiona can't give you any answers."

"Bit hard to do that when she's in ICU in a coma." Lance refused to back down, making their encounter a clash of the titans. "She's the fifth attack this week. We've had three die on us, and the other two have no memory of what happened to them."

Was this in addition to the supernaturals being killed? I couldn't ask him if one was a brownie. Lance was ignorant of the magical world and a norm. "If they suffered a head injury, it's likely they won't regain their memories." Brain damage was tricky and impossible to heal. I'd bet whoever was responsible took steps to ensure their victims couldn't talk about what happened. I wondered why they left humans alive but realized they wouldn't pose a threat to their plans.

It was clear the being responsible was able to pass for humans so they could move around so freely. I set that aside to consider another time. "Who died? I haven't heard anything about these incidents."

Lance proceeded to tell us about the two victims found behind the bar where Aislinn worked and the third in the parking lot of Mug Shot, the café owned by Bruce, a dwarf. The fourth victim was discovered not far from Violet's bookstore, and then there was Kendra.

It chilled me to discover the attacks occurred within hours after I had visited each location. I didn't tell him that. No freakin way did I want to be hauled in for further questioning. I was clearly the uniting factor but couldn't share that with him.

"I wish there was something I could tell you that would help. I don't know Kendra, and the others aren't familiar either. Violet was really the only friend from my childhood that I kept in contact with and remained close to, so even if I knew them at one point, I lost touch long ago."

"Have you tried asking Mae or Camille to use their psychic gifts?" Violet's voice was like a bomb in the room. At least, that's how it felt to me. Although everyone stopped moving to stare at her for one incredulous second. Thankfully, Lance missed the silent concern.

Was it too early for wine? This day wasn't shaping up to be any better than yesterday. I grabbed the chocolate croissants Bas picked up the night before and put them on a plate before setting it on the counter.

"You know I don't believe in that stuff," Lance grumbled as he set an empty mug down.

Violet wagged a finger at him. "You should know better than to say that. Especially in Isidora's house." I then noticed Grams floating through the walls with a determined look on her ghostly face.

I waved my hand, trying to force her to retreat before she was seen. Lance's brown eyes settled on me with a furrowed brow. "What's wrong with you?"

I choked on the pastry that stuck in my throat. "Wrong pipe. But Violet's right. My Grams taught me the power of insight. Mae and Camille might have the information they can share with you."

Lance sighed and grabbed a croissant. "Mae told me everything she knows, which wasn't much. And I doubt

Camille will be able to say anything to give me a direction for the investigation. I need solid evidence. And fast. There's someone stalking residents of our town, and it's my job to stop them."

Aislinn straightened from the wall where she'd been leaning. "It's a shame you have such a narrow mind and are so dismissive. Psychics are very helpful and often able to tell you where to start looking. Last week Camille helped Fiona find Is...uh, a necklace from Isidora. Turns out it was in the house the entire time but hidden. Without her assistance, it would have taken us far longer to discover."

She'd been talking about how the witch helped call my Grams to me. I doubted I would have ever been able to successfully bridge the veil between the living and dead to pull my grandmother across it and back home without her.

At that moment, I wished I was a seer and was able to glimpse the future. It would have come in handy a million times since I moved to Pymm's Pondside. It would be nice to be psychometric, too. Then I could ask to see the picture or even go visit the woman and see what happened to her with the brush of my hand.

There was plenty of evidence to suggest a bilge was responsible for the killings, but that didn't explain the fact that humans were injured and killed, as well. Surely, they would have suffered a worse fate. From what I'd been told, the Dark Fae creatures showed no mercy. I saw evidence enough of that at Tunsall's house.

"You act as if they have magic or something. Finding a lost piece of jewelry is far different than discovering who tortured and killed people. It doesn't take a genius to suggest looking behind dressers or under tables or something similar. Usually, when something like that is lost, it's because it was knocked off of where you set it down."

Clearly, Lance didn't believe magic or witches or

anything of the sort existed. I'd even go so far as to say he found the mere idea ridiculous. It couldn't be easy for him to be responsible for a town where more than half of its inhabitants were real creatures of myth and legend.

"I see you aren't willing to stretch your imagination and give something new a try. So, why do you think she was carrying my picture? Should I be worried? After all, you said she had a gun, too." I was trying to piece together the information.

My gut told me they switched things up when I enhanced the wards. I'd bet the humans could fool the protections and get past the boundary. And then there was the fact that I proved I could use my power to detect a Fae's presence. It meant they couldn't sneak up on me like before.

"I'd say she was working with someone that has it out for you. Only it doesn't make sense. From what I was able to discover, you lead a simple life with minimal strife. Your biggest issue was when your husband got sick and passed away. Nothing that would have created enemies. The director of nursing at your hospital said you were never listed in a complaint or malpractice suit." Lance ran a hand through his sandy blond hair.

"So, what you're saying is you think there is someone that wants to hurt Fiona, and you can't protect her." Sebastian's words landed like blows on Lance's shoulders. As the Chief Constable, he felt responsible for what happened in his territory. "Don't worry, Constable. I'll be sure to do your job and keep her safe."

I had no idea why Bas was goading Lance, but it wasn't helping. I stepped in between the two men and pinned Sebastian with a glare before I turned to Lance. "Thank you for stopping by. I know you have a million things to do today, and trust you will let me know if you discover anything new."

I gestured to the exit and waited until Lance nodded to Violet and Aislinn, then left my house. Conversation stopped the second I reentered the kitchen. Grams was right behind me. "You need to go see that woman. She knows who set her up to kill you. We need that information."

I thrust my hands on my hips. "What exactly do you think I am going to do? She's in a coma. It's not like I can talk to her."

"Not with that attitude. You need to stop thinking like a norm. A simple dream spell will get you inside where you can direct her mind." My grandmother stopped by the island and looked longingly at the teapot. I imagined it must be hard for her to be incorporeal. It made her presence even more of a gift.

"I'm not sure leaving Pymm's Pondside is such a good idea," Aislinn interjected.

"Why's that? We need the information." I hated sitting there doing nothing. My hands burned with my power bubbling right under the surface.

"I think it's a setup. A stranger walking around with a weapon and your picture would get the authorities' attention. And yours as well. Of course, we would want to go and question her. Anything to lead us to whoever did this. It's the perfect trap. We'd walk right into it unsuspecting."

Violet gasped. "You're right. And it took several tries for whoever did it to get it right, which is why there are the other victims."

"Good point. We stay here," I told them.

Sebastian shook his head. "Not all of us. I'll go and see what I can learn. Argies you can come, as well. If they show their faces, it'll be better to have both of us there."

I didn't like the idea of putting them in danger, but it was better than walking into a trap. Besides, the two men were more than capable of defending themselves. Everyone kept talking about how powerful I was and how much more I would gain, but I couldn't see how I would ever have more than Bas and Argies.

CHAPTER 18

"*W*hat precisely is toadstool? Is that like frog poop?" No way was I going to drink anything that had fecal matter in it.

Grams glared at me from under her bushy eyebrows. "Don't be ridiculous. Why would you use something that can give you a deadly bacterial infection? It's actually a type of mushroom."

Aislinn laughed, and Bailey chuckled from her spot on the window seat in the attic. Violet's daughter hadn't gone far from our side since we rescued her. I knew she was shaken but hoped this didn't ruin her desire to strike out independently. Every child needed to leave the nest and test their wings before they could truly fly.

Violet entered, holding a platter of sandwiches that she set on the table opposite of me. I'd added another to the attic because I had no desire to eat from the surface I used to create potions. I was terrible, and there was always something overflowing my beakers. I had visitors daily, so there was a real chance I would end up ingesting something that would hex me with genital warts or something.

"Don't forget the stardust," Grams warned, "or you will end up blocking your energy instead of joining a dream."

"Where the heck is the stardust?" I scanned the shelves and couldn't find it.

Aislinn joined me with a hoagie in hand. "Whose fantasy world are you going to enter? Sebastian's?" She waggled her eyebrows while she chewed.

I considered telling her Argies, but I suspected something between the two, and I didn't want to come in between the possibility of love for her. She deserved someone who thought the moon and sun shone in her eyes.

"I haven't thought about that yet. I wanted to practice my potion making and thought this would be a good one in the event we needed to use it."

Grams pointed at me. "You need to stop doubting your abilities. It inhibits your progress to a significant degree. You're a nicotisa and capable of more than any witch or Fae in the past century."

I shifted my feet and looked away. I didn't like the pressure of being so powerful and what others would expect of me. "I shared with Violet and Aislinn. Doesn't that mean I'm not as strong?"

"No. It has had the opposite effect. You have even more, as do you two," Grams explained to my surprise. How could that be? I gave it away. How did I have more? "However, it isn't as easy to detect you or your level of power. If I hadn't felt it myself, I would doubt what you are now."

"That makes no sense. How is that possible?" Logic told me I should have less, not more, after sharing it.

"What about Violet and me? She feels more powerful to me. And my connection to the elements is far stronger than it ever has been. Not to mention my spells have as much power as if I were a full-blood." I'd never heard Aislinn discuss herself like this.

I had wondered at the tone her voice took when she mentioned being a half-blood Fae. If I had to guess, I'd say she experienced discrimination at the hands of someone for being less than at one point in her life. It was a poignant reminder that women everywhere, regardless of their magical status, were told they weren't good enough unless they had a pixie-sized waist, enormous breasts, and flawless skin.

The worst part of that was the suffering was mostly self-imposed. It wasn't as if people went around telling me outright that the extra bulge around my middle and the crow's feet at the corners of my eyes were horrendous. They didn't need to when every ad on TV and in magazines contained images of perfect women. It was really driven home when you were passed up for that promotion by someone a decade younger even though you had far more experience.

I was done with doubting myself and my abilities. And, I'd make damn sure my friends believed in themselves, as well.

"You both have been elevated. And thank the Gods for that. It's about time this town was run by some competent individuals. Camille and Mae just weren't powerful enough to break through the barrier and join the council. I expect more from you three." Sometimes it was as if Grams could read my mind. It was exactly what we all needed to hear. I could see the impact on Aislinn as she straightened and smiled wide.

"Taking on this council will have to wait. We have a killer on the loose and a realm to save. Although, I have no idea how we are going to do either."

Violet turned from Bailey, who was gazing out the window while listening to our conversation. "We need to capture the bilge. It's the surest way to identify whoever is behind all of this."

"We already know it's either Thelvienne or Vodor. I say we eliminate the assassin and go after them. It'll kill two birds with one stone. We can remove them from power, stopping their machinations and free Eidothea at the same time." I nibbled on a sandwich as I considered how easy it was for me to talk about taking the lives of the bilge and the King and Queen.

"You must not assume Vodor or Thelvienne are behind the attacks. There are plenty of Fae and witches that would love to steal your power." Grams' warning made the hair on the back of my neck prickle. I didn't like thinking others had it out for me, as well.

"She's right," Bailey announced as she turned away from the window to look at us. "I never once sensed any royal magic when Ben and I were taken. If either were responsible, the Fae would have carried their signature, and they didn't."

Violet knelt by her daughter and cradled her hands. "Were you able to detect anything that will help us identify the culprit?"

Bailey shook her head from side to side. "The magic wasn't foreign. It felt like Cottlehill Wilds, but I must have been wrong."

Aislinn started pacing around the attic. "There are plenty here that have complained about escaping one tyrant to find themselves with even more restrictions here."

Grams waved one hand through the air, leaving a trail of white in her wake. "I doubt you're wrong. Fae that escaped Vodor's grasp expected to be able to live openly and freely when they moved here. It's the reason the council was formed, to begin with. We live side by side with norms and need to remain hidden, or we will suffer a worse fate."

"True. I just wish Dereck wasn't head of the council. He's a pompous, self-important jackass," Violet complained.

I hadn't ever met Dereck, and from that description, I didn't want to.

Grams pursed her lips and narrowed her eyes while she turned red around the edges. "He's a real piece of work. I can't wait until you three oust him from his position. I've been searching for a way to get rid of him ever since he and your father got into it. I still swear he is partially to blame for you growing up away from here."

I opened my mouth to ask more about that but shut it when I got a ping from the portal. It wasn't as insistent as I had experienced before. "I need to go deal with whoever is at the portal, but I want to hear more about that when I get back."

Grams returned to her regular whiteish-blue coloring throughout. "There's not much to say. He saw your dad as a competition for the head of the council and didn't like it. Remember to use your connection to the land to help you determine the Fae's intent. If they mean you harm, the magic will warn you."

"Right. It'll feel like something is trying to cut me off. I remember feeling boxed in and removed from the elements right before that last one pulled me through the portal. I'll be back."

Grams continued asking Bailey questions about what she'd seen and felt as I took my leave. I hurried down the narrow staircase, anxious to get this over with. I passed Ben, who was rummaging in the fridge.

The cold snap of the early evening bit into my bare arms. I shivered and wrapped my arms around my waist. That's what I got for leaving the house without a jacket in the early winter. It was uncomfortable enough that I turned and grabbed a sweater from a hook in the mudroom.

Steam rose from the pond, telling me Kairi was regulating the water's temperature. I recalled the frozen water from childhood visits. There was no doubt in my mind that Kairi would prevent the surface from freezing over now that she lived there.

The energy of the portal greeted me like a familiar friend. Ever since I traveled through it, I felt closer to the magic for some reason. Before, I had been able to ignore the summons without much effort. It was separate from me.

Now there was this feeling deep in my gut that I couldn't ignore. I suspected even if I hadn't experienced the call before, I would know without needing to be told. And under it, all I knew, whoever was there meant me no harm. That didn't mean I let my guard down, though.

Entering the crypt, I saw the oval window into Eidothea and was greeted by a smile on a handsome face. I knew better than to trust those dancing green eyes. I stood close to the entrance and waved a hand, erecting a bubble around me that would prevent being yanked through if he managed to get close enough to touch me. My magic came with ease and precision. Kinda nice to see I was making some progress.

"Well, hello there." Was he flirting with me? I still wasn't used to men hitting on me. I thought of Sebastian and Argies as the odd ones. After all, it had been years since anyone had shown much interest in me. Then again, perhaps supernaturals had a far different taste. Or maybe he just wants your power. There was that.

"I'm guessing you want passage to Earth. Why is that? Are you fleeing Vodor?" I didn't have time to play games at the moment and continue the game of seduction. There were bigger fish to fry.

"I'm Finarr." His dark brown hair started blowing around his face at that moment as if it was swooning over his stunning eyes. "And I am a friend of Sebastian. Is he around? I need to talk to him."

Not what I was expecting. "Are you a friend of Argies, too?"

He lost his smile and narrowed his eyes. "What do you know of Argies?"

It didn't take a licensed therapist to detect his mistrust. "I met him when I was pulled through to Eidothea. He helped Bas get me home and came with us."

Finnair's shoulders slumped, and he exhaled. "That's a relief. It's about fucking time something went our way. I was coming to ask Bas to return and take Argies's place. The rebellion can't maintain without a leader organizing things and keeping hope alive."

"Would you like to come through?" I surprised even myself with the offer. "They should be home soon."

He inclined his head. "I've never actually been to your realm, but I am curious. More about you than anything else."

I smiled and granted permission, extending a hand to him. His fingers breached the veil, and when he clasped my hand, I tugged on his soul. He instantly stumbled forward and crashed through the portal head-first.

"Fuck," he cursed as he landed on his back then rolled across the ground. I heard shouting behind me and turned to see some mounted patrols charging toward the portal. Instinctively I removed permission and commanded the veil to close. In a bright flash, it winked out of existence.

"That's a handy feature to keep the King from getting to you. I knew you had it easy here on Earth."

I glowered at Finarr and headed for the door. "Far from it, asshole. I moved to Pymm's Pondside six months ago. It's been one fight after another with very little time spent relaxing or even learning how to use my magic."

Finarr threw up his hands. "I meant no offense, and I had no idea. No one in Eidothea knows about that. Word is that

177

you managed to injure Thelvienne because you're rested and have had time to perfect your defensive skills."

Finarr glanced around us and his gaze traveled over the foliage before sticking on the tombstones. It made me think about how I had never seen anything resembling a cemetery in the Fae realm.

"We're on my family's burial grounds. I used to think it was creepy to bury our dead so close to home, but now I understand that it's to keep our power close and help protect the portal with generations. According to my grandmother, our family's blood and bones offer far stronger bases than anything else. It's also why they built the mausoleum using the skulls of my great-great whatever. And I haven't mastered anything. You're lucky you weren't burned upon entry. I start fires more often than anything else."

My internal radar went off again, telling me someone was on my property. I was really coming to like that feature of my magic. I looked to the long driveway hoping it wasn't Lance again. I couldn't deal with him again today.

When Bas's truck came into view, something in me settled. I had been on edge since Grams died, and I took over. The only time I wasn't all wound up was when Sebastian was close. That connection with him kept me from indulging in Argies when I had the chance in Eidothea.

Finding someone you had such a close affinity for was rare. And I never expected to have it again after I lost Tim.

I lifted my hand and waved at the surly guy who'd captured a piece of me when I wasn't paying attention. As usual, he scowled and narrowed his eyes before they focused on Finarr.

After parking the vehicle, he jumped out, followed by Argies. "What's happened? Why are you here?" Argies's voice was agitated and carried more than a hint of worry.

"I came here to talk to Sebastian about returning. Shit is

falling apart. No one knew where you went, and it was assumed Vodor's men killed you."

Bas crossed his arms over his chest. "I'm not leaving while Fiona is in danger. Argies isn't either."

"As much as I want to drag you both back, it's probably better that we stay here and protect her. Thelvienne was seen leaving the castle three weeks ago," Finarr informed us. My blood froze in my veins. I scanned the area where I faced her before.

I suddenly felt exposed standing out in the open like that. "She's coming after me. I told Grams she was the one sending the bilge after me." I was already walking to the back door.

I heard their footsteps behind me but didn't pause to look back. Violet and Aislinn were in the kitchen when I entered. "The Queen left the castle weeks ago and is probably out there hunting me as we speak."

Sebastian came up behind me, his presence comforting me like nothing else could. My mind had already worked itself into a panic. It was whirling in a million different directions, trying to find a way to keep me safe.

"How do you know?" Aislinn asked around a mouthful. The platter of sandwiches had been brought down, and she had a half-eaten one in her hand.

Argies closed the distance to Aislinn and gestured to our latest guest. "Finarr told us."

"Is this the one that came through the portal just now?" Grams' voice echoed before she appeared. When she materialized next to him, Finarr shouted and jumped back, bumping into the island.

"Yes. He's a friend of Sebastian and Argies and came because the rebellion in Eidothea needs help." I flicked on the kettle to boil some water for tea and started the coffee maker.

Violet thrust her hands on her hips. "We need the protection and help. Especially now if the Queen is back and hunting you, too."

"I told you, I'm not sure Thelvienne is behind the recent attacks," Grams admonished Violet. "We can't be sure there isn't more going on. She's a nicotisa and a major target for any power-hungry idiot."

Finarr shifted wide eyes from Grams to me, then to Sebastian, who placed his hands on my shoulders. "She's the one destined to save us from Vodor's cruel rule."

Bas lifted one corner of his lips and snarled at Finarr while Argies shook his head at the guy. "I had the same thought when she appeared on my doorstep. I can't say for sure, but she has agreed to return to Eidothea and assist with the fight."

My mind whirled. Argies had mentioned something similar when I was at his house. It seemed there was some kind of prophecy out there saying I was the Fae savior. It had to be wrong. I was no hero. Hell, I couldn't even work my magic correctly.

"But she's not leaving now. There's a threat to our town that needs to be dealt with." Grams' tone brooked no argument. And there was no arguing with her when she got something in her head. "Sandwiches aren't enough for four grown men, Fiona. You need to make them a meal while we hear about what's going on in Eidothea."

Case in point, I didn't even try arguing with her. I had no desire to cook, but I turned to the pantry anyway, unable to tell her I wasn't cooking. It was bad manners to leave guests untended. She'd taught me that, and it seemed the lesson refused to leave despite my magical new life.

Grabbing corn shells, ground cumin, and canned beans, I turned to grab some ground meat from the freezer. Tacos weren't precisely formal, but they were quick and easy. Not to mention delicious.

Sebastian silently approached and helped by chopping tomatoes and lettuce for toppings. My hand lifted and caressed the charm at my neck. It hummed with power and was a symbol of the bond I shared with the guy. The closeness I felt to him brought back images of him kissing me.

That quick, my body heated, and arousal flooded me. I had been ignoring how much I wanted from Bas. The way my body came alive under his touch told me I wouldn't be able to ignore it much longer. And I didn't want to. Waiting was pointless and only denied us. I wasn't betraying Tim by being with Sebastian.

I looked up and to find Bas's heated gaze focused on me. I swallowed when I saw the promise in their depths. It's about damn time. My rational mind chose that moment to rear its head reminding me I was still uncertain about being intimate with him.

When my hormones were at the wheel, I was ready to throw caution to the wind and get naked. My body was more than ready for playtime, but I wasn't entirely on board. I no longer had the body of a twenty-something. My nipples pointed south, I had more stretch marks than a road map, and my thighs resembled a mountain range. I wasn't sure I was ready to reveal myself to Sebastian.

CHAPTER 19

"So, you think she has more than one person after her?" Bas went to the fridge while he spoke and grabbed a roast from the freezer. Apparently, he was helping me cook. Thank God for that. I wasn't sure what I was going to do.

Going with his choice, I grabbed the contraption my daughter bought me for Christmas that was a pressure cooker, only it plugged into the wall. I emerged from the pantry and set it on the counter, and went back to grab some more ingredients.

"Of course, there's more than Thelvienne and Vodor after her. Everyone with so much as an ounce of magic felt when she broke the spellbinding her magic. Be sure to add some beef consume, Fiona," Grams instructed me, then continued talking about the mess I currently found myself in. "No doubt it attracted every thief and sleazebag in the country."

Aislinn set her mug down. "How will everyone know what that was? I had no idea until you explained it to me. I tried to find out if Vodor had done something. It was the only explanation that made sense to me. There aren't too many that have enough power to hit me with a wave from their magic."

"It even reached Eidothea," Finarr added. "It was shortly after the pulse that Thelvienne left the realm, and Vodor sent out a summons."

"How does he think stealing power from his subjects will help his reign? He's killing his kind. Soon enough, he will have no one left to rule." I tried to dampen my frustration, but the growl was evident in my voice.

Bas dropped the roast and some veggies into the pot. "Vodor is an idiot. He has never considered the consequences of his actions. He discovered how draining someone else would elevate him centuries ago and can't stop now, or he risks losing his position. For a being like him, the thought is untenable."

"To drain another is despicable," Argies bit out. His disgust was warranted but made my stomach cramp.

I couldn't help the memory of being flooded with power when I killed the Fae after being pulled to the Fae realm. I didn't mean to take his power and never intended to kill him. I was as bad as Vodor. I could never let my friends or Grams know what I'd done. And I prayed that it never happened again.

Argies continued talking, unaware of my internal crisis. "More and more of our kind have retreated below ground or sought refuge on Earth. Eidothea is crumbling around us, and we can't stop it without help."

Finarr turned his gaze to Bas. "The King is coming unhinged. We don't have much time, and you know Fiona is the one that will turn the tide in our favor."

I held up my hands. "Okay, stop right there. Why everyone so convinced I am supposed to help save Eidothea? I might theoretically have this superpower, but I am not the person an entire species should rely on." My chest was heaving as I struggled to catch my breath.

Grams reached out but her hand passed through my shoulder, leaving a chill in its wake. "I tried to save you from all of this. Your parents, too. None of us wanted you to be the target of so many plots or carry this burden. I would share this with you if I could."

Violet gasped and shifted her gaze from Aislinn to me. "But we can. We're connected now and by more than a coven name. Aislinn and I will share this burden with you. You aren't alone anymore."

Emotion choked me, bringing tears to the backs of my eyes. I had been blessed in my life. I never realized how much until recently. Grams and my parents sacrificed everything to ensure my safety. I suspected Grams even lost her life because she was protecting me. And I had the best of friends. Violet had always been there for me as a sounding board, and now she and Aislinn were willing to share a massive burden with me.

"Fiona, you're surrounded by many people there to help you in your journey. I see now that I was wrong to protect you from the inevitable," Grams admitted. "We need to discover who has been killing Fae lately. Like I said, I think someone else is after you, Fiona. What are the chances that Thelvienne has come here? And, do you think Vodor would leave Eidothea to seek Fiona?"

Sebastian ran a hand through his hair. "Thelvienne is a vindictive bitch. She never lets anything go and holds the grudges of all grudges."

"He's right," Argies agreed as he leaned against the arch leading into the living room. "I'd say Thelvienne is making her way here as we speak."

"Where is the nearest portal? Do we have time to set up a

trap of our own?" If I could get ahead of her this time, I might be able to beat her.

"Vodor closed all of the portals in Eidothea when he discovered Thelvienne had left the castle. Rumor has it she refused to give him an heir, and they've been fighting over her threat to gain enough power to overthrow him…and win you back." Finarr locked gazes with Bas as he spoke. The reminder that the Queen was in love with Sebastian made something twist in my chest. I wanted to teach the vile woman a lesson or two.

Bas waved a hand through the air. "That's never happening. I think we need to call a meeting with the council. They can set up alerts throughout the city and outlying areas. It'll give us time to prepare."

"If we know when and where she arrives, we can direct her to a trap," Aislinn suggested.

Violet bobbed her head. "We can set it out of the way where no one will get hurt."

"I doubt the council will help. They're a bunch of assholes." I'd never heard Grams sound more bitter.

Sebastian chuckled, but it was a menacing sound. "They'll have no choice in the matter. Camille is on our side, so she can help sway the others to see things our way. And we can enlist them to help search for anyone else hunting in our town."

I wasn't sure they were right to involve the council, but it was worth a shot. I didn't have any better idea. I was ready to cross one enemy off my growing list of things to do.

* * *

A SOFT KNOCK sounded at my door. "Come in." My voice was barely above a whisper. I had no desire to rouse anyone up or let my Grams know I was awake. She'd had enough to say the night before.

It was Sebastian that twisted the knob and poked his head inside the room. The sight of him was nothing less than striking. He was a God-made flesh, far beyond my reach. Unfortunately, that knowledge didn't stop my yearning for a second.

"I wasn't sure if you were up or not." He was adorably uncertain as he glanced around and bit his lower lip.

I sat up then realized I was in bed in my pajamas. My hand flew to my head and tried to smooth the tangles in my hair. He pushed the door further and crossed to my side in a rush. My jaw dropped when I caught sight of his bare torso and the cotton pants on his lower half.

My stare got caught on the muscles in his chest, He was a perfect male specimen, and the sight of so much skin had my lady bits tingling and warming with need. "Are you okay?"

I finally snapped my mouth closed and ran my hand across my mouth to make sure there was no drool there. "Ummm, couldn't sleep. You?"

A soft chuckle broke my concentration, and I looked up at him. He was smiling at me as he walked to the door and pushed it closed. The heat in the room went up twenty notches. Great time for a hot flash. It was too much to hope. It was just my desire taking over. I knew better at my age.

"I was up patrolling and swear I could hear you thinking."

"You think you know me so well," I teased. How the heck did he know I was up perseverating on the meeting I was having with the council the next night?

A shiver shook his frame, drawing my attention back down. His nipples pebbled, making me want to run my mouth over his flesh. As Grams used to call it, my *lady place* grew moist, and my core ached to be filled by Bas. I nearly forgot all the reasons I wanted to take things slow with him.

I forced my eyes up, and we locked gazes, staring at one another for several seconds. Sebastian's nostrils flared, and his eyes reflected his desire. "I know you better than you think. And right now, you want me."

"Wh…what?"

His body moved like liquid sex as he made his way back to the bed. "You want me to kiss and lick and…"

"Okay," I blurted, jumping to my knees and lunging for him. He was close enough that I didn't end up on my face on the floor. It wasn't a graceful move. I fell into him, and my hand pressed over his mouth.

His lips curved up in a smile, and he ran his tongue over my fingers. It was my turn to shiver. I sank back on the heels of my feet and tried to take a deep, calming breath. All that accomplished was bringing his woodsy, masculine scent to me, making me melt into a puddle of arousal.

"Before we get to the kissing," he paused, and I was up and pressing against his chest in a flash. My mind went blank as his arm wrapped around my middle and pulled me tight against his body. "Are you alright? Tonight was a lot. I think you always suspected someone else was after you, but hearing your Grams confirm those fears made it real."

I sighed and lowered my forehead to his shoulder. His strength and heat surrounded me, making me feel safe. All it took to banish my fears was his presence. "I'm not alright, but it doesn't much matter. I'll meet with the council tomorrow night and get their help discovering who else is killing Fae in town while I set a trap for Thelvienne. By the way, you have awful taste in women."

Lifting me up, he sat down and pulled me onto his lap. "I don't know. I've picked at least one incredible woman."

Heat infused my cheeks with his insinuation. I couldn't bring myself to ask if he was talking about me. It seemed impossible. "You make it really hard to think straight."

"Then don't. Just forget about everything for the moment and let yourself go."

I stared into his eyes and wanted nothing more than to say yes. But under the cotton t-shirt and shorts was a sight that was sure to cure him of his erection in an instant. I tried to roll off him, but he held me tighter.

"No. Push everything outside the two of us out," the command in his voice was undeniable and irresistible.

It intoxicated me, and before I knew what I was doing, I was yanking my shirt over my head with a smile on my face.

"Gods, you're gorgeous," he growled.

My arm came up and covered my boobs. My face turned down, and I tried to get up again. I had tossed my top, and I had no idea where it was, or I'd already have it back on. "Don't hide from me." His tone was rough, and his desire was evident.

"It's been a long time since anyone other than my late husband saw me without clothes, and I'm a couple decades past my twenties."

"You are perfect, Fiona. I am not asking for you to give me something you aren't ready for. But know this. I want you and no one else."

I wanted him, but I knew better than to get naked around him. Flimsy as they were, I needed the barrier of my shorts and underwear. I shifted my weight and gasped. It wasn't just his muscles that were big on his body. His cock was long, thick, and very hard at the moment.

"I don't think I'm ready for this. I rely on our friendship for too much right now to risk everything for sex. I can't do any of this without you."

Bas ran a hand over my jawline and cupped my cheek. "You don't have to worry about that. I will always be by your side regardless of anything else."

His hand moved down my neck and across my shoulder.

There was no fabric to impede his progress. I didn't give any physical resistance when he pushed my arm away from my chest. He didn't go for my breast like I expected. The teasing touches he peppered me with had me practically writhing in his arms.

When his hands settled on my hips, the contact sent little licks of arousal straight to my core which was pressed over the bulge in his pants. I took a deep breath, and my nipples brushed against his skin, titillating me, but it was his moan that made me still.

I looked up and realized he hadn't meant for the noise to escape. It was primal and full of need and desire. I couldn't quite comprehend that I was affecting him as much, if not more than he was affecting me. It was exhilarating to have a sexy guy like Bas be so turned on by me.

Testing my theory, I wrapped my arms around his neck and lowered my head to his. Electricity zapped me when our lips touched. The kiss started out slow and quickly heated up. Before I knew it, I licked my way into his mouth and kissed him soundly.

I was panting by the time I broke away from his mouth after. My chest was heaving as I tried to catch my breath. A groan left me, and he barked out a curse when my nipples brushed over his hard pecs.

"Holy hell." His breath hit my cheek with each harsh word.

I felt his erection jerk against my swollen clitoris. My arousal was so high all it would take was a few seconds of rubbing against him before I exploded. I would be embarrassed, but I was too busy trying to dampen my desire.

Wanting to tease him in return, I lowered my hand to grab him through the cotton pants. Before I made contact, he had flipped me around and pressed my back against his chest. One arm a solid band around my flabby stomach. I scrabbled against his arm to push his touch away before he felt how out of shape I really was.

"This is too much." The more my thoughts raced, the further I was pulled from the mind-numbing arousal coursing through me.

His head lowered to my shoulder. "It's okay. Neither of us is ready to go that far. All I want to do right now is alleviate some of your stress," he whispered against my ear. His tongue traced around the shell, making me shudder.

This time when I twisted out of his embrace, he allowed it. I stood there, refusing to cover my breasts. It was clear he wanted me, and I refused to hide for the rest of my life. As difficult as it was to have his gaze scan me from head to toe, I stood still while he got a good look. When I had sex again, it would be with someone who appreciated the blemishes and imperfections. They were a part of me and not going anywhere.

Bas growled low in his throat. I couldn't help but check him out, as well. My eyes flew wide when I got a glimpse of the tent in his pajama bottoms. My wrists were grabbed. I glanced up when he pushed my arms above my head. His eyes were glued to my chest since the move pushed my breasts out. Amazingly enough, they barely sagged in this position.

He ran his tongue over his bottom lip, then looked into my eyes while he gathered both hands in one of his and palmed one of my hips. My apprehension was erased when his touch traveled from my hip and dipped below the waistband of my shorts. All that stood between his skin and my slick entrance were my cotton panties. One of his long fingers plunged beneath the elastic of my underwear and grazed me. My hips punched forward, wanting more. With one touch, he had me in the palm of his hand.

"That's it. Forget about everything but my touch." He

punctuated his statement by slowly tracing a circle around my quivering flesh, driving me crazy. I nearly grabbed his hand and forced it to where I needed it most. The fact that this was the most erotic moment of my life because of his teasing touches and focus on me kept me rooted in place.

"What about you?" I wanted harder pressure. I wanted more than his fingers, but I wasn't sure I was ready to take things that far. It wasn't a simple matter of being afraid anymore. It was the changing dynamics. This was far more than sexual pleasure between two consenting adults. If we went there, one or both of us would fall hard for the other. That is what frightened me more than anything. There was no doubt I would fall for this guy in a heartbeat. The last thing I needed in the middle of my magical midlife crisis was to get heartbroken.

Sebastian leaned over with my wrists trapped in one of his hands and ran his tongue over my nipple. At the same time, his finger finally delved deeper. "Oh, God, yesss," I hissed.

His deep brown eyes scalded me when he looked up from my breast and gave me a sexy half-smile that almost made me climax. The grin alone was something else, but the sight of him hovering above my hard nipple smiling was erotic as hell.

He kept his eyes on me as he bit down on my pebbled flesh. Each nip zinged straight from my breast to my core which he hadn't stopped teasing. It took every ounce of strength I had to keep from grabbing his thick arousal. It was a hot, heavy presence against my abdomen. I did lift one leg and wrap it around his hips. It brought his erection close to the finger, teasing my slit.

"Please don't stop. I'm so close." I wasn't above begging. My body had never been wound this tight. My magic buzzed beneath the surface like I was a bottle of champagne he'd shaken up. I briefly wondered what would happen when I finally climaxed. It was entirely possible I could blow the roof off my house, and I didn't care. I wasn't about to ask him to stop now.

Bas straightened and brought his mouth close to mine, then released my wrists. My fingers twined in his thick brown hair while he played over my body. He grabbed one of my breasts, squeezing it at the same time he inserted a finger into my core.

My hips moved on their own. Each movement brushing against his cock. I didn't stop to think about what I was doing. Pleasure had taken over my brain. His shaft pulsed through his soft pants, and I pressed myself against him while my pleasure built.

His fingers became rougher on my sensitive female flesh, and his moans were just as loud. He was as lost in the moment as I was. My body was coiled tight. I was close to climaxing and began to ride his hand, taking what I needed. Never in my life had I acted so brazenly. Not even with Tim. There was something about Bas that made me lose my mind entirely.

The muscles in my abdomen tightened, and my sheath squeezed his finger before the world exploded behind my closed eyes in a wash of bright lights. I pressed my leg harder into him and let my body ride the wave of pleasure. I collapsed to my mattress in a boneless heap, and he sat down beside me.

"Fiona!" My Grams' voice shattered the moment and stopped me from reciprocating and giving him the release that he so clearly needed.

Sebastian groaned and ran a hand down his face. "I need a cold shower." He went into the bathroom connected to my bedroom while I tugged my shirt over my head.

Doors all along the hallway opened by the time I made it

to the hallway. So much for trying to keep her from waking the entire house. "It's about time you got up. We need to practice some spells before you meet with the council. No witch is going to force her way into your head if I can do anything about it."

"What? You never said they'd try to force their way into my head, Grams." I knew I was shouting, but I couldn't help it. I had a hard time focusing on what she was saying while still coming down from an incredible orgasm.

"It's six in the morning, Isidora. What the hell?" Aislinn griped. I noticed Argies standing in the room behind her but kept my mouth shut.

"I'll make some coffee." I ushered everyone to the stairs so they didn't see Bas leave my room. I wasn't ready for the questions. Hell, I didn't want to overthink it. As predicted, I was falling for the guy and had no idea what to do with the emotions. Dealing with homicidal maniacs was far more straightforward.

CHAPTER 20

*T*gaped at the scene before me. "I can't believe you live with this view, and we've never hung out here and practiced spells." Aislinn's house was right on the cliffs and had a perfect view of the ocean below. The sound of the waves was soothing as my nerves jumped beneath the surface.

"That's what you're worried about right now?" Aislinn stared at me with her hands on her hips.

I lifted my shoulders and let them fall. "Better than the alternative."

Sebastian came up behind me and rubbed my shoulders. I wished our time together this morning hadn't been cut so short. My body tingled when I remembered the release he'd given me.

Violet paused next to me. "Fiona's right. Next girl's night, we come here. I love your view." It was great to see the weight lifted off my best friend's shoulders. It had nearly killed me when Ben and Bailey had been kidnapped. I couldn't begin to imagine the toll it had taken on her. Despite all that she'd gone through in the past few days, she was still at my side, ready to help defend me and our town.

"They're meeting us at the cove," Camille informed us with a shuffle of her feet. Despite my Grams' dislike for her, the woman had given me training when I had no one else. "You first, Fiona. The stairs are over here."

I followed Camille's finger and took a deep breath before heading down the steep staircase. I hadn't been to the beach since moving to Pymm's Pondside. Violet and I used to race each other down this steep incline and spend hours playing in the water and on the sand. It was a vastly different experience being there now. It was freezing and didn't seem nearly as fun as I recalled.

Of course, that was in large part due to the cold weather and slippery steps. Not to mention the fact that I was about to face this mysterious council for the first time and demand they do something to help hunt down whoever was killing in Cottlehill Wilds. Based on my Grams' grumblings about corrupt assholes and Camille's insistence, they were all-powerful, capable magic users. I wasn't sure what to expect.

The second both my feet hit the sand below, the world around me blurred and shifted. The dizzying array of colors that swam around me had my stomach-churning. A groan slipped from my mouth, and I turned back to brace myself on the rail. My palm hit the wood, but Sebastian wasn't behind me.

Forgetting about the way my head still spun, I glanced around frantically for my friends. "Bas! Violet! Aislinn!" My voice seemed to hit a wall where it was absorbed before going anywhere.

What the fuck was happening? Was the council isolating me from my friends? That would make sense, but Camille wasn't there, and she was the group leader. The air crackled around me and made the hair on my arm stand on end. My long locks had been pulled into a ponytail to keep it out of my face. I could feel the ends frizzing on the back of my neck.

I'd been through enough to know the knot in my gut meant something evil lurked nearby, and I had stepped into a trap. My magic surged forth when I called it. The second the vile female waltzed out of the cliff face, a ball of lightning escaped my hand and zipped toward her head.

Thelvienne tsked me and wagged her finger at the same time she waved a hand and sliced through the spell before it reached her. I growled when my magic fizzled and died before it landed.

I tossed a couple more to have the same thing happen. With my chest heaving and my mind whirling, I balled my hands and held my magic back. "Congrats. You managed to get the drop on us. But it won't last."

I taunted her hoping to distract her while I searched for the spell keeping my friends outside the bubble she'd created. If I could find it, I would be able to blast it away so they could help me.

"What makes you so special?" The words flew from her mouth along with spittle as she growled at me.

I smirked at her knowing it would enrage her further. When you got mad, you tended to make mistakes. And I needed her to make a whole lot of them if I was going to make it out of this alive.

"I like to think it's my shining personality, but Violet is convinced it's my thick head of hair."

"You think you're so funny. I can't believe Sebastian finds you attractive at all. You're crass and have no class. Look at you. You're a mess." She waved her hands up and down while pointing at me.

I didn't need to look down to agree with her. I had on jeans that were too tight because I was bloated from the wine we drank the night before. My sweatshirt was tighter than a sausage casing, and my hair looked like I'd put my finger in a light socket. All those insecurities that had nearly paralyzed me the night before came rushing back.

Don't listen to that perfect prima donna. Bas didn't give a fig about any of that. He thinks you're perfect the way you are: lumps, bumps, and all.

"You might be right, but he doesn't see it that way." I didn't manage to say anything else as she screamed at me and threw a ball of fire at me. I dove to the side and ate a mouthful of sand and still hadn't managed to avoid being hit.

Fire slammed into my side and singed my clothes and skin. The agony was blistering and stole my concentration for a second. The flames licked higher and were about to reach my tangled hair by the time I finally pulled my head from my ass and cast a water spell.

The deluge poured over me and splashed onto Thelvienne's pristine velvet gown. The blue darkened where the water hit the fabric. It was oddly satisfying to see the Queen lose some of her shine.

Stop gloating and get to it, Fi! Right. I was rolling to the right before I bothered looking around. When the sand exploded where I had been a moment before, I was grateful for my inner monologue.

Time to go on the offensive. Surging to my feet, I tossed a bludgeon spell in the direction she had been. A grunt told me I managed to hit her. It wasn't the scream I had hoped for, but it was something and bought me enough time to check my side.

Wet warmth trickled down the side that had been burned. My gag reflex punched the back of my throat, and I nearly lost my lunch when I caught sight of the burned flesh. It was a blackened mess with red bits of meat and muscle here and there. And it was bleeding steadily.

I staggered and threw my hand out and barely caught myself on the rocks behind me before I ended up on the ground again. The air prickled again, and I jumped to the top of the rocks right before Thelvienne's spell hit the stone and blew it up.

I watched almost in slow motion as rocks flew toward my face when the dark light hit the stone below my feet. Unsure what to do, I leaped at the waves crashing two feet from me. Saltwater hit my side, and I was the one screaming as the burn stole my focus.

The spell I had coiled in my palm fizzled like my burn. I choked and started coughing as I inhaled more than my share of the ocean. A hand fisted in my hair and yanked me out of the water.

"Time to end the distraction you pose. It's time Sebastian came home with me. Don't worry, I will put your power to good use and kill my husband with it."

My scalp stung, and my side hurt. I shoved the discomfort into a box and scrabbled to get my feet under me. The water receded, making it easier to stand up. The Queen still had my ponytail in her hand, so I couldn't get to my full height, but I didn't let that stop me.

My magic surged with my slightest urging. Razors. The thought popped into my head, and the spell was out before I could censor it. It blasted through the hand I'd grabbed her middle with. It was her turn to scream as blood peppered my face a second later.

Reaching up, I pried her hand from my hair and tossed her aside. The Queen didn't go very far. She snagged the tattered side of my sweatshirt, her nails raking through my burned flesh. Forgetting magic for the moment, I balled my hand into a fist and punched her in the side.

My hand came away bloody, and she let go of me. We stood glaring at each other for a second before she narrowed her eyes. She looked as bad as I had to at the moment. Her dress was in tatters, with her abdomen and back bleeding from a dozen cuts. Even her hair was no longer the sleek black waterfall but was now a tangled mess.

The Queen's fingers sparked, and she threw what looked like a black sparkler at me. I called my magic and threw a spell at her. I wasn't entirely sure what I conjured, and a second later, I was on my back after the black energy slammed into my left shoulder.

All I could hear was my panting and the frantic beating of my heart. I tried to lift my hand and throw another spell, but it never moved. I was vulnerable, so I diverted my energy to covering my body with a protective bubble while I caught my breath. I needed to keep her from landing another blow. I wouldn't make it if she managed that.

I managed to turn my head. My breath caught when I saw her lying there in a heap of blue velvet and blood. One of her legs was bent at a wrong angle, and her mouth opened and closed as she tried to catch her breath, but her chest had a gaping hole in the middle of it. The edges charred black.

I watched the light go out of her intense green eyes. I hadn't even registered that I killed the Queen when that green light separated from her body and lifted into the air. The wind whipped around me as her power zipped toward me.

It slammed into my chest, making me gasp. I hadn't been mistaken before. I had absorbed the Fae's power, and I'd just done it again. Only, I had no idea how I did it. I never meant to, but that didn't matter. It was done. And my friends and Grams would never see me the same again.

The world around me came alive in a rush, and I blinked up into familiar deep brown eyes. I tried to get up, but Sebastian pushed my chest down. "Don't move. You're hurt badly."

"I didn't mean to," I blurted.

Violet fell at my other side and grabbed my hand. "It's okay. She needed to be taken out. She had evil plans for her realm..."

"And Bas," I added, cutting her off. "But I took her power." I couldn't hold back anymore. I needed my friends to know. I would rather they hate me now and walk away than in the middle of a crisis.

"That's not possible," Bas said as he looked at me with a furrowed brow.

My breathing was still erratic, and I hurt all over, but I finally managed to lift to a sitting position. "But it happened. I didn't mean to. It just happened like it did with the Fae at the portal."

Finarr nudged the Queen's body. It was starting to shrivel up right before our eyes. None of the other Fae bodies did this when they died. "The King will have felt her death. This will no doubt set him off. He will be out for your head, Fiona."

Sebastian jumped to his feet and was in Finarr's face. "Don't threaten her."

Finarr lifted his palms up in the universal sign for 'Woah, calm down. "It wasn't a threat from me. You both need to know Vodor will be out for blood after this. I mean he was after her before. Now I'm fairly certain he will come after you eventually."

Bas took a step back. I wanted to get up and go to him, but I couldn't move. Violet wrapped her arm around my shoulders. "We will deal with that, but we need to figure out what is going on with Fiona. I can feel how much more power she has now. We need to know why she is absorbing a Fae's power." I leaned into my best friend. I was immensely grateful she didn't hate me at the moment.

Aislinn shifted next to Argies. "I felt a surge right before the spell was shattered, as well."

Violet's mouth turned down at the edges. "I didn't feel anything. Did you guys?"

Bas glanced at me for several silent seconds before shaking his head from side to side. "I felt her agony, but nothing beyond that."

My eyes flew wide. He'd felt my pain? "How did you feel what I was going through?"

He shared a look with Argies and Finarr. "I'm not entirely certain. We need to deal with Thelvienne's death before the King comes after you. Block the connection you have to her now."

"I don't..." My voice trailed off without finishing my thought. The denial about to leave my lips would have been a lie. I had no idea I was connected to the Queen. I quickly cut that thread and enclosed myself in a bubble. Only I wasn't in it alone. Sebastian, Violet, and Aislinn were there as well.

Violet stood along with Aislinn. They both helped me to my feet. "Now what?" Aislinn asked. "Do you think the King will be confused by all of us being part of her circle?"

Camille blew out a breath. "We need to get the Queen through the portal before her body poisons the waters here. And, we need to find the council and make sure they aren't still under some spell."

Finarr bent and lifted the mummified corpse from the ground, and Sebastian picked me up in his arms and started back to Aislinn's house where our cars were parked. "I think there's a good chance the King won't be able to pinpoint Fiona thanks to her connection to us all," Finarr postulated.

"Isidora can help us with next steps after we toss her body through the portal," Violet said as we reached the top of the staircase.

"I won't put you guys in more danger." I refused to have any of my friends hurt because I couldn't control my magic.

"You aren't in this alone, Fiona. We're the Backside of Forty, and we are in this together," Aislinn promised.

"Yeah," Violet agreed as she held open the door to Bas's truck. Finarr jumped in the back with Thelvienne. "We're a coven. One of us is in danger. We all are. Right now, there is nothing you need to do except rest and recover after you open the portal."

If only it was that easy. I may have eliminated one threat, but I put an even bigger target on our backs in doing so. My eyes were heavy, and my side hurt like a bitch. I was going to pass out any second now, and my friends were in danger. My heart started racing, and my finger itched to do something to protect them.

Sebastian set me on his seat and climbed in beside me. "I will not let that asshole anywhere near you, Fiona. Being the subject of someone's rage is nothing new to us. Yes, Vodor will be angrier, but Violet is right. You need to heal. We will deal with this soon enough. You will be no good to any of us if you aren't at your best."

"Okay." I laid my head on his shoulder and shoved all my fears into that little box, and locked them up. They were right. I had to heal so I could ensure none of them were hurt in the process.

Don't forget you're a badass now. Your magic reacted as an extension of your mind without much prompting. You'll be ready for Vodor. I had to be. The lives of those I loved were on the line.

gh! Nastiest thing in the universe. I didn't want to touch the Thelvienne's body. It resembled a dragon-sized prune rather than the beautiful woman she used to be. My body was still thrumming with energy as I had yet to integrate all of the Queen's magic in with my own.

My heart had yet to settle from Indy 500 levels and my mind was trying to analyze the how's and why's of my magic. Unfortunately, I was never able to figure anything out. And it made me feel like Ron Weasley. Never able to recall spells of the theory behind them.

I went back to wondering why Thelvienne withered like she did. None of the other Fae I'd killed had done that. And the ground was indeed being infected. The ground started sizzling where her blood had splashed. Putrid smelling smoke drifted into the air while the foliage turned brown around the edges.

"Alright. We'd better get her through the portal. Pymm's Pondside doesn't deserve to be poisoned by her." I bent and choked as bile rose in my throat.

Aislinn wrinkled her nose. "I love being part of the Backside of Forty, but I think I might draw the line at handling the festering raisin lady."

Bas huffed and lifted the Queen as if she didn't weigh a thing. "I've got her. You'd think you hadn't just killed her or something." He directed the last part at me. Despite the body he was carrying, heat sizzled between us.

I hadn't allowed myself to consider sharing my life with anyone else ever since my husband, Tim died. He was my first love and always would be. I was happy focusing on my work and my kids until I had my magical new beginning six months ago.

Now, I found myself considering options I could never have even dreamed of. Sebastian was irritable, gruff and didn't have a romantic bone in his body. But he was also sex walking with muscles on his muscles.

I shook my head at him as I shoved the distracting thoughts away. "I wasn't trying to kill her. Hell, I would have run away screaming if I'd known I was going to absorb her energy. I get the feeling that fact is going to bite me in the ass."

I saw my grams looking out the window above the sink as we passed into the family cemetery that was on my land. I could see right through her ghostly form to the clock on the wall that told me it was well past midnight. *That* was why I was exhausted right down to my bones, *not* because I am a forty-five-year-old hybrid Fae-witch with a bad knee.

A sound rumbled from Bas's chest as he walked beside me. "Is that an invitation? I'd love to bite your delectable bits. But we should be concerned Vodor's anger that his mate was killed."

My body heated and my mind shut off as I listed to his deep voice. It made me think of nakedness and compromising positions. Heat filled my cheeks and I spluttered for a response. Sebastian didn't mince words and usually said what was on his mind, so I wasn't certain why his comment had me so flustered.

"You might want to watch it, Bas. She might scald your twig and berries." Aislinn's warning was followed by a round of laughter. The sound of my friends' amusement jolted me and highlighted the reason for my discomfort. Having my friends hear intimate desires made me want to crawl in bed and pull the covers over my head.

Maybe I really was a prude, but I didn't want anyone knowing what Bas wanted to do to me. And I most certainly didn't want anyone knowing how badly I wanted it. Somethings were best left to private moments.

I hauled the door to the crypt open and looked back at Aislinn. "Can you hold this open? Once we toss her through, I'm going to take a shower."

"Got it," Aislinn said as she placed a hand on the stone panel.

I walked into the space and looked around at the bones of my ancestors that made the foundation of the portal. Lifting my hands, I chanted the spell to open the portal. An oval hovered in the middle of the room with light surrounding the area. I saw the familiar Fae world of Eidothea through in the center of the oval of light. Seeing a scene of another world in the middle of a crypt where dead people are buried was surreal every time that I encountered it.

After the dark Fae had forced the portal open and tried to sneak through to Earth, I was glad it was back to only opening when I gave the mental command. The bright green, almost neon really, grass was beautiful, and I could smell the sweet scent of flowers carried on the breeze through the opening.

"Throw the bitch through," I called out to Sebastian over the sound of wind whipping through the small building.

Bas chuckled and approached the portal then threw what

looked like a mummified husk through. I winced when it landed on the grass. It instantly started smoking and turning brown. When the acrid smell started replacing the sweet floral scent, I closed the portal.

Turning, I brushed my hands together and walked out of the mausoleum. "We need to regroup before you guys head home. I desperately need a shower, but I can see grams isn't going to let that happen."

The ghost of my dead grandmother was glaring out the window with her arms crossed over her ample bosom. She wore one of the hideous tops covered in flowers that she loved to wear. The v-neck kept the fabric away from her throat.

I recalled being a little girl and asking her why she wouldn't wear the cute lavender sweater I'd gotten her for her birthday. She told me there was no way in hell she was putting anything on that would constrict around her waddle. She explained that the fabric would choke her, get caught on her chin hairs, and put the extra skin on display.

My hand rose to the skin that was just starting to loosen on my neck. Some days I wish I was that naïve young woman again. When my finger hit something hard and prickly, I lowered my head. I had to at least go to the bathroom and pluck the ugly black hair that had a magic all its own.

Seriously, how was it I would rip the little shits out one night and the next morning it was back and nearly three inches long!

Bas held the back door open for me. Grams floated in my direction immediately. "What the hell happened out there, Fionna?"

"Not now Grams. I need to use the restroom." I fled up the stairs and slammed the door the second I entered the bathroom connected to my bedroom. Opening the top drawer, I grabbed the tweezers and thrust my chin toward the mirror.

Gah! I couldn't believe I was fighting the Fae Queen looking like the bearded lady. My grandmother floated into the room when I was gripping the second hair between the metal.

"You cut me off to pluck your chin hair?" My grams couldn't be louder or sound more irritated.

In my rush to shut her up, I tugged hard than necessary then lifted my eyes and sent her a glare. "Would you be quiet? I don't need the entire house hearing I need to shave like a man."

Grams rolled her eyes. "Whatever just happened is going to alert any supernatural across both realms. I want to know what the hell went down out there. I couldn't see anything from the windows."

I yanked the remaining hair out and washed my hands. That's what had her up in arms. I imagined it was difficult for her not to be able to get involved with their battles. Grams had never been shy or one to sit idly by. Part of the reason I was so fierce was because I was her granddaughter.

"I'm sorry about that, but it couldn't be avoided." I opened the door and descended the stairs to the first floor. The house was large for a cottage in the countryside. And it was open for being built centuries ago.

The familiar creek of the sixth step and the family pictures on the wall at the base of the stairs helped center and calm me. Everyone was in the kitchen. "You are a Goddess," I praised Violet for making a pot of coffee.

"You never did develop a taste for a proper cuppa." Grams's usually complaint was another comfort. This was why I chose my magical new beginning here in this house. I was surrounded by history and family that helped ground me in any storm. It was also why I fled her right after Tim had died years ago. The three weeks the kids and I spent here helped me face life without Tim.

"You taught me to enjoy tea, but there are times I cannot survive without the blessed dark brew and this has been a rough night." I inhaled deeply, savoring the roasted coffee bean scent.

Grams had her arms right back over her chest and one hip cocked to the side. Emotion clogged in my throat with the sight. For longer than I could remember, my grand-mother had needed a hip replacement. She'd fallen in her garden and broken it when she was seventy-eight and it never healed quite right.

To see her sass back as she took her demanding pose was fantastic. "What the hell happened out there? Why did I feel this wave of dark magic ripple through the house? There was no real power behind it, so it made no sense."

I was right back to my childhood and shuffled my feet like I used to when I was trying to avoid telling her that I messed up. "Well, remember when I told you about absorbing that Fae's power? I kinda killed the Evil Queen and her powers floated into me. My blood turned to cham-pagne in my veins and energy buzzed through me then spread out to Aislinn and Violet," I told her and continued to describe how her body withered and we tossed her back like she was a fish we didn't want to keep.

Grams's blue-white shape solidified enough that I could no longer see the sofa in the background. "You've landed in another mess, Fiona. Vodor will not let this go. Thelvienne was his life."

The most unladylike snort left me. "I cannot believe she was anything to him but a pain in the ass. They fought constantly and word on the street was they hated each other."

"Hate and love are often intermixed. I have no doubt he

didn't like her but being with her allowed him to strip crea-tures of their power. He would never willingly give her up. His need for her was so great that he overlooked the fact that she was in love with Sebastian and pined for him for centuries. No man in his position would be able to do that if he could live without the woman."

Hearing about Bas's previous girlfriend made my stomach twist into knots. I knew it was ridiculous, but I couldn't change it. I was barely able to hide that fact from my expression.

I chanced a glance in Sebastian's direction and noticed he was scowling at my grams as he sipped from a glass of amber liquid that was no doubt scotch. "I need to check with the council and see if they have any insight."

Camille set her glass in the sink and turned back to the group. "I'll go with you, as well. I'd like to hear what they have to say, too."

In the end Finarr ended up joining them which left me, Aislinn, Argies, Violet and my grams in the kitchen. When the coffee was done burbling and pitting out liquid gold, I poured myself a cup and added plenty of sugar with a splash of cream.

"D you have any idea how we should handle the King, Grams?"

My grandmother floated to the window over the sink and looked outside. "There is nothing safe for you three to attempt. Vodor has too much power. You might be a *nicotisa* but you are still learning your craft and what you're capable of. I tried to find as many books and scrolls on the topic as possible, but all there seemed to be were cautionary tales."

"We can't sit around while he kills innocent Fae, Grams. Besides, we won't be facing him alone. Argies and Bas's parents are part of a massive rebellion in Eidothea." I implored her to listen to reason, but she only shook her head which sent her silver hair flying around her shoulders. I looked like waves crashing around her body.

Argies opened his mouth to say something when my internal alarm system pinged me. Groaning, I took another sip of my coffee then set the cup down. "I'll be right back. I'm being paged."

Grams was in front of me in an instant and was red around the edges like when she was angry. "You will not go out there, young lady."

My mouth fell open and I stared at her for several seconds. This was so completely out of character for her and I was at a loss for words. My grams was serious about her role as the Portal Guardian. So much so that she set up a spell so I could bring her back from the other side.

At the time I had no idea how any of it was possible, but I'd learned enough through various conversations that it wasn't simply a matter of having unfinished business. Grams had to cast spells on herself that went soul deep. That's what I ended up calling back was her spirit.

That was nearly unheard of. The rebellion in Eidothea had been hunting for centuries upon centuries for a way to cast a spell on a soul. That was the way they felt they would beat Vodor. Their realm was losing its magic and would soon enough be out entirely. No one wanted to think about that possibility.

"Why would you say that to me? I *have* to answer the summons."

Grams had her hands on her ample hips as she narrowed her eyes at me. The look made me feel like I'd disappointed her. It was something I had never handled well. Anytime I got that look I tripped over myself to make it better.

"You just killed the second most powerful being in the Fae Realm and you want to go say Hi? I thought I taught you better. You got sucked through last time you tried to repel a dark Fae."

Her words stung and my mouth immediately wanted to snap *You didn't teach me shit. That's why it's been one battle after another since I discovered my magic.* I bit that acerbic comment back and took a deep breath.

"You taught me to never shirk my duties. I'm the Portal Guardian now. What if it's someone like Kairi who is being hunted by the King's men? I have to go see who and what it is." I softened my tone, hoping she heard the respect I had for her and her opinion.

Grams's chest heaved as if she was panting, but she made no noise that indicated she even breathed. "I have been doing this a very long time, Fiona. Whoever is trying to get through means us harm. And you would know it if you paid attention to your summons."

"Fair enough. How can I tune into intentions without being face to face?"

Grams lifted her head and smiled at me. "Follow the summons back to its source. You know it's the portal because of experience, but you can trace it back and discover more."

Closing my eyes, I tried to do exactly what she said. Nothing happened which didn't surprise me at all. The intricacies of performing magic hadn't come naturally to me. Once I figured something out though, I was able to cast the spell or access the source with ease, so I tried again. The second I latched onto the trail energy blasted through it and slammed into me.

I felt my body fly through the air at the same time dark energy scalded my veins. It hurt like a bitch and made me cry out. My eyes snapped open and I saw the island pass below me. My heart struggled to beat, and my lungs wanted to shut down. Before my mind could catch up with what was happening my back hit a corner and a loud crack filled the room.

Argies was somehow in front of me and catching me before I hit the wood floor. Tears streamed down my face as I tried my hardest to suck in a breath. My lungs felt like deflated balloons in my chest.

Grams was in front of me and Aislinn and Violet were shouting something. Argies carried me from the kitchen and to the living room. I cried out with every step he took. "I'm sorry, Fiona. Hang in there until I can set you on the couch."

"She's bluer than you are, Isidora. What do we do?" That was Violet's frantic voice.

"Join hands and cast a spell to force her Fae side ascendant. It will heal her lungs before she dies."

I heard my friends shout, "*Ascendant* Fae." Warmth surrounded me at the same time Argies set me on the soft cushion. It caused sharp pain to slice through my chest. I swear my heart stopped for several seconds.

Thankfully within seconds the pain lessened enough, and I was able to take in small gasps of air. Violet and Aislinn knelt in front of me with Argies and Grams behind them. It took an eternity for me to suck in a full breath. The pain was horrendous, but it no longer threatened to make me black out.

"What…the…hell…was that?"

Grams had a frown on her face. "It was a trap like I was worried about. Vodor is powerful indeed if he was able to hit you through a source, he shouldn't even be able to access."

Sweat covered my body and nausea churned in my stomach while the pain receded at a snail's pace. I was entirely too old for this crap. And unprepared for this magical twist. Even if I wanted to go back on my promise to help fight Vodor it wasn't possible now.

He could reach me without ever leaving Eidothea. Guilt

rose to join the party of nausea, agony and bile. He was likely making innocent Fae pay for me killing the Queen as I laid there struggling to stay alive.

"I'm sorry for questioning you, Grams. I don't think I would have survived if I'd gone into the crypt."

"You might not survive the night. He managed to take out most of the protections Pymm's Pondside that have been built by countless generations of Shakletons."

I sat up so fast I couldn't even stop myself. Black spots danced in my vision and I lost my battle with bile, throwing up all over my lap. A decade later after the heaving died down, I wiped my mouth with the back of my hand.

"Looks like we need to rebuild those first. I'll just need a minute." Or a year. That would work much better, but I didn't think the Evil King would allow me the opportunity.

ABOUT THE AUTHOR

Authors' Note

Review are like hugs. Sometimes awkward. Always welcome! It would mean the world to me if you can take five minutes and let others know how much you enjoyed my work.

Don't forget to visit my website: www.brendatrim.com and sign up for my newsletter, which is jam-packed with exciting news and monthly giveaways. Also, be sure to visit and like my Facebook page https://www.facebook.com/AuthorBrendaTrim to see my daily posts.

Never allow waiting to become a habit. Live your dreams and take risks. Life is happening now.

DREAM BIG!

XOXO,

Brenda

Araton (Dark Warrior Alliance Book 22)
Cambion Lord Araton (Dark Warrior Alliance Book 23)

Dark Warrior Alliance Boxsets:
Dark Warrior Alliance Boxset Books 1-4
Dark Warrior Alliance Boxset Books 5-8
Dark Warrior Alliance Boxset Books 9-12
Dark Warrior Alliance Boxset Books 13-16
Dark Warrior Alliance Boxset Books 17-20

Hollow Rock Shifters:
Captivity, Hollow Rock Shifters Book 1
Safe Haven, Hollow Rock Shifters Book 2
Alpha, Hollow Rock Shifters Book 3
Ravin, Hollow Rock Shifters Book 4
Impeached, Hollow Rock Shifters Book 5
Anarchy, Hollow Rock Shifters Book 6

Midlife Witchery:
Magical New Beginnings Book 1
Mind Over Magical Matters
Magical Twist
My Magical Life to Live

Mystical Midlife in Maine
Magical Makeover

Bramble's Edge Academy:
Unearthing the Fae King
Masking the Fae King
Revealing the Fae King

Midnight Doms: